E. W. Irving

WITNESSING THE KILLING OF EMILE POMET

BY

E. W. IRVING

E. W. Irving

Copyright © 2023

ISBN: 979-8-9908000-0-7

This society is not likely to become free of racism, thus it is necessary for Negroes to free themselves by becoming their idea of what a free people should be.

– Ralph Ellison, Working notes to *Juneteenth*

Author's Note

This novel is a lamentation over Black ghetto life in the United States. Avoiding religious themes and allusions, it echoes the jeremiadic tradition of Black authors before, during and after the Antebellum. Instead of focusing on white racism as the major source of present-day Black misery and dehumanization, the narrator laments ghetto dwellers' own complicity in their dire condition and fate through their silence, surrender and inertia. The story is not an indictment per se. Rather, it is an earnest plea for introspection and corrective action.

1

Driving to an interview for my Sunday newspaper column, a puff piece, I witnessed a murder. More than a hundred other people also witnessed it. I was there because I had stopped for gas at the Arab-owned station several blocks from the site of my interview.

Having finished pumping gas, I heard the loud profanity.

"Who you fuckin' wit', muh'fucka, huh? Who you fuckin' wit'?"

I parked at the curb. The journalist in me had kicked in as I watched the frantic activity behind Cue

Man Pool Parlor, a business in the Mall of African Peoples. I turned on my phone's video and mic and trotted toward the commotion.

The wiry thug in his late teens, wearing a huge gold chain around his neck, sagging cargo pants and a knitted Rasta hat, shouted at the handsome, well-dressed Black man in front of him: "Who the fuck you, muh'fucka? We Gut Bucket niggas."

He punched the well-dressed man in the face with such force that the man stumbled backward, dropped his yellow legal pad but somehow stayed on his feet and adjusted his tinted eyeglasses. He glanced at his gold wristwatch, bent down, retrieved the legal pad and brushed it off on his trousers.

Rasta gaped at the man's poise.

"I don't want trouble," the man said. "Just conducting business."

I recognized his French accent as that of the Haitian upper class. He backed away and brushed himself off.

In his mid-fifties, he was handsome, fair-skinned and had the thick wavy hair most American Blacks covet.

He held his bearing as Rasta stepped toward him. He was one of the unflappable types I regularly met in Port-au-Prince when I was there to cover the aftermath of a 7.0-magnitude earthquake.

"You don't know us, nigga," Rasta said, his shoulders and arms and hands and head moving in *that* stylized way.

Many other thugs had gathered, all resembling little boys in sagging pants and exposed underwear, oversized T-shirts, clownish head coverings and untied sneakers. Jaded young women stood behind the thugs.

The crowd urged on Rasta, and it seemed that every phone in the lot was filming the action. I hid behind a knot of old men. Although few people in The Gut Bucket read the newspaper, especially the opinion pages, I could not risk being recognized. I put on my sunglasses, held my face down and looked up only when I had to pick my way between sweaty bodies.

Another thug, his massive black dreadlocks down to his waist, walked from the pool parlor and shoved Rasta aside. Dreadlocks wore a colorful dashiki, cargo pants, sandals and a monster-size gold chain around his neck. His physique was muscled, his amble that of a cheetah. His very presence silenced everyone near him.

Rasta stepped away from the Haitian. My video rolled as Dreadlocks pulled a Glock 19 from his dashiki and aimed at the Haitian in that sideways thug manner. The Haitian raised the legal pad as a shield. Dreadlocks fired. The pad flew into the air. The round hit the Haitian in the chest, knocking him back several feet.

He clutched the wound, stunned at seeing his own blood oozing between his fingers. He stared at Dreadlocks and sank to one knee. The front of his sky-blue shirt had turned red, and he struggled to stand but could not.

A horde of more onlookers materialized. Dreadlocks fired a second shot, hitting the Haitian's stomach. Blood gushed and pieces of flesh and fabric sprayed into the air. The Haitian fell backward, settling on the ground on the side of his heart.

I eased to the front of the crowd, my video running. I could see the Haitian's handsome face and vacant eyes as he reached out and muttered a name I could not understand. He muttered the name several more times, reaching out and gasping.

A Well-Dressed Pretty Woman, a few feet from the dying man, screamed and ran away in terror, her hair in curlers.

Rasta stood over the Haitian.

"Don't never dis Gut Bucket niggas."

The skinny teenager next to Rasta wearing a Miami Dolphins hoodie and dark glasses kicked the

Haitian's temple. I was struck by how young Hoodie was. He had a child's face, which made the viciousness of his kick surreal.

How can a mere child be so cruel? I thought, sure that he would spend the rest of his life, probably a short one, hurting and killing fellow Blacks.

He kneeled and took the dying man's gold watch, then tried but failed to remove the wedding ring. He stood, put the watch on his wrist and held it up.

"Worth about three hundred dollars," he said.

Dreadlocks glanced at the watch and rolled his eyes.

"Dumb ass. Try three or four thousand."

"Muh-fuck!" Hoodie said, looking at the watch and grinning.

Slapping hands, he, Dreadlocks and Rasta strutted back inside Cue Man. As the crowd encircled the body, I eased to the front. The body lay there, the wedding ring and shiny black shoes glinting in the sunlight, the handsome face smeared with dirt and blood.

Although I had covered many killings in the ghetto as a police reporter, I could not describe what I felt as I looked at the dead man. It was not shock or fear or anger. Staring around at the animated faces of witnesses, I was ashamed to be of the Black race, and I was profoundly humiliated as I heard familiar terms of endearment: "brother" and "bro" and "bruh" and "sister" and "sistergirl" and "cuz" and "homie" and "blood" and "OG" and "dawg" and "my man."

The absurdity of the camaraderie reminded me that nothing in Hell was endearing. I thought of Bruegel's 1562 painting *The Triumph of Death*. In it, I saw a version of the Black ghetto: a forsaken landscape with doomed creatures suffering and dying, lost in ignorance and indolence, trapped in crime and hopelessness.

Two white cops wearing bullet-proof vests exited

their vehicle and approached the crowd that had grown to at least three hundred.

"Popo!" a woman screamed. "Popo!"

The cops moved cautiously, no one willingly giving an inch to the "white muh-fuckin' pig muh-fuckers," as someone yelled. I wondered why young white men would risk obliteration in The Gut Bucket. A paycheck? A desire to hurt or kill Blacks? To gain respect among their peers as a means to rise through the ranks? For sure, it was not to "serve and protect."

"Anybody see how this happened?" the taller cop asked, his Cracker accent contemptuous, his face carrying that familiar *fuck-you-niggers* expression. "Anybody?"

A man yelled, "Muh-fucka got his ass lit up."

The crowd roared, high-fiving and slapping hands, and the cops stared at one another, shaking their heads and sneering.

Scattered among the adults, several preteens and

teens stood like statues as they looked at the dead man. A Young Teen Girl leaned over the body and whispered. I moved close to her but could not understand her. The man's blood oozed into the dirt in a pool that resembled a Rorschach inkblot, and some blood soaked into the legal pad beside the body. Young Teen Girl lowered her face and hurried away. I kept my video rolling as the cops tried but failed to solicit useful responses in the crowd. They shut their notebooks and muscled their way through the crowd to their cruiser.

I walked around the mall, the unofficial "Black City Center." A Pan-African flag always flew on a pole out front. The mall was a strip of five small shops. Besides Cue Man Pool Parlor, there were Just Ribs restaurant, Aces High Barber Shop, Blessed Life Beauty Salon and On the Rocks Liquors. A mobile bail bonds office was always parked in its reserved spot for clients who came and went all day every day except Sunday.

The buildings were owned by Seed of Africa, an association of self-styled liberation groups that claimed in its mission statement that "Black People, except Uncle Toms, are descended from African Royalty." No Black person, including me, ever publicly challenged the ridiculous claim. Leaders of the group, all handsome dark-skinned men, wore traditional African clothing, and all had adopted Swahili names, Akida, Hami, Jabali and so on.

Green-and-gray mold streaked from the buildings' rooflines to the ground, and the surrounding air was malodorous, especially after heavy rainfall. The place would have been razed years earlier if it had been anywhere else in this otherwise idyllic city on the Atlantic coast.

An ugly irony was that the mall was an official site on the African American Heritage Trail that touted Black achievements to curious whites who ventured there on their own or who rode the city tour bus. I could always distinguish foreign tourists from Americans. Invariably, foreigners showed genuine interest and asked serious questions of the tour guides while American whites mostly smirked and whispered.

Six makeshift canopies rimmed the parking lot. Every day, men played cards and dominoes, drank knotty head gin and fed their narcotic habits in the shade of the canopies. Two portable basketball hoops stood in their special section of the lot, which was designated the "African Peoples Free Zone." Even cops, especially whites, stayed away until summoned by a Black elected official or if a building caught fire or if a white female went missing and was reported last seen there.

On Saturdays and Sundays, from sunrise to sunset, Seed of Africa operated a profitable community market in the lot, selling everything imaginable: from jerk chicken, to wedding dresses, to used vehicles, to hand-churned ice cream. Whores connected with "dates," and a smooth-talking conjure man sold good fortune, curses, dolls and voodoo pins.

A well-dressed preacher performed "laying on of hands" for generous donations. He always had long lines. Every Sunday afternoon, unless it rained, several couples jumped the broom, surrounded by cheering relatives and friends and curious out-of-towners.

The five square miles around the mall were appropriately called The Gut Bucket, a warren of cheap buildings, trashy yards, filthy alleys and junk-filled cul-de-sacs manned by drug dealers and their enforcers. Ironically, a church was in every other block. It also was home to Canal Park, two acres of green space and recreation equipment, so named for the putrid canal that traversed the area and drained four miles away into Rainbow Basin, a massive retention pond that kept flood water away from condos for elderly retirees.

Building contractors, Black and white, regularly dumped their construction waste in Gut Bucket alleys because, according to conventional wisdom, even among Blacks, "Niggers don't give a fuck about their own neighborhood, so why should anybody else give a fuck?"

More cops and the medical examiner and his all-white team arrived. Behind the ME came Karl Murray, one of two Black city commissioners. Weighing some three-hundred pounds, he was a locally born-and-bred enabler of all that was wrong in The Gut Bucket, too often valorizing thugs and portraying them as victims of "the system."

What rankled me most was that he was the pastor of a three-thousand-member church, and his influence and popularity were wide, making him one of the richest Black pastors in South Florida.

In a Sunday column, I referred to him as "a merchant of bull poop" and "an ordained charlatan." Although my editor let my insults go into print, the publisher, having endured Murray's "cancel-subscription" rant and threat of a lawsuit, insisted that I go to the commissioner's office and apologize. Buzz in the newsroom was that Murray was running for mayor next election, and he had an excellent chance to win.

I went to his office in city hall, and he scolded me the moment I sat.

"Your negative write-ups keep businesses from investing in our community," he said. "I don't understand why you tear us down and don't lift up your own people."

Although I wanted to be cordial, I would not let him get away with scapegoating me. "Commissioner, you know less about business than I do. Serious investors hate violence and chaos and filth and loitering. They don't need my 'write-ups.' There are only a handful of profitable Black-owned businesses in The Bucket. Arabs own the places that make the big bucks, and they don't invest here. We traipse like automatons into their filthy stores, and we can barely understand a word the cashiers are saying while we hand over our cash like fools. Don't blame my 'write-ups' for that." My disgust grew the longer I looked at him. "Even Blacks with money won't invest in The Bucket. The new Black-owned business, that ladies fashion boutique, is downtown, three miles from where we're sitting. You blame me for that, too? Why didn't these three Black women open their shop here in The Bucket? You know the answer, but you're too intellectually dishonest to acknowledge it."

"Why can't you be like other Black reporters?"

"You mean be a sock puppet to be accepted?"

"What I meant --."

"I know what you meant. I'm not your kind of

Black. You can't tell me how to be Black, commissioner."

"It's not about how to --."

I cut him off. "Have you been to the drugstore on Third Avenue?"

"Not recently," he said sarcastically.

"It has a sheltered bus stop with a bench. Old people and the handicapped get off and on the bus there for their meds. It's their lifeline. The only drugstore in The Bucket. But that shelter stays full of trash and smells like piss and puke. A bum's always curled up on the bench, and the people have nowhere to sit. I talked to the store manager two weeks ago, and he said they're closing that store next month. Too much liability. Theft. Loitering. You know about that?"

He fidgeted and said nothing.

"There won't be a drugstore in The Bucket," I said.

"People will have to travel five miles for their

scripts and pay for taxis and Uber, which most can't afford. The Black employees will lose their jobs. You know what else? The Bucket is a food desert. The nearest grocery store's six miles away. You okay with that?"

He looked at me as if he had chomped into a green persimmon.

"No, it's not okay."

"Then what're you going to do about it? This is your district, your parishioners."

He stood, balancing his bulk with one hand on the desk. "You writing about this?"

"No."

"Whether you do or not, you don't come in here and talk down to me."

"Actually, I came to apologize for that insulting column I wrote. I'm sorry for what I wrote, and I'm sorry that we got off on the wrong foot."

"Mr. Clary, you really need to pray."

I was tempted to reply with a lecture on prayer's inefficacy, but I did not because I had followed my publisher's order to apologize. Murray let go of the desk and stood up straight, his giant gut poking out.

"You're not a member of the Divine Nine are you?" He said.

"I'm not into secret handshakes, step shows and branding."

"Our frats and sororities are more than that. They're service and philanthropic and academic organizations. Brotherhood and sisterhood. Loving our people, Mr. Clary."

"Let's just say I'm not a joiner – of any kind."

"Not even a church," he said as a reckoning.

"Not even a church."

His shoulders slumped and he sighed. We never spoke again.

I recalled that old encounter as I watched him walk through the crowd, a path parting like the Red Sea for his massive frame that was stuffed into a navy blue Brioni suit.

He stopped near the Haitian's body, not looking at it, and raised both arms for silence. I stayed out of his view.

"Good people, good people, here we go again, another misfortune," he said. "We have to stop this. It's embarrassing me. At the last commission meeting, I asked for funds to buy new equipment for Canal Park, for our children. This incident won't help my efforts." He glanced at the body and surveyed the multitude. "Good people, I don't want to come back anytime soon under similar circumstances. My office door's always open, and you know where to find me."

"Yeah, the fuckin' chow line!" a young thug yelled to the hoots, fist-bumps and high-fives of his comrades.

Murray laughed and waved with both hands. I was surprised that he did not launch into his signature bellicosity and recitation of Bible verses. He walked into the mass, shaking hands and patting backs. I realized again that the hypocrite was beloved.

As he approached the rear door of Just Ribs, Eugene Tilden, the sixty-year-old owner, greeted him and led him inside. The crowd milled around the Haitian's body a few more minutes, lost interest and sauntered away.

Smothered by the sun's overbearing heat and the clash of funky body odors, perfumes and colognes, I chose to disappear. My being dark-skinned was a plus because Black people are so color struck that we automatically dismiss the presence of dark skin, making anonymity advantageous for a Black journalist in The Gut Bucket where we were despised for being Uncle Toms and Judas niggers.

Easing out of the crowd, I saw two white paramedics covering the Haitian's body. Their precise and respectful motions were alien to this place, and I wondered if they, like me, were repelled by the horror of what had unfolded. Or were they robotic professionals who would return in a few days to remove another body and transport it to the morgue?

2

Driving to my interview with Ella Pierce, director of the Black Diaspora Museum in The Gut Bucket, I relived the killing and became nauseated. I pulled to the curb, grabbed my phone and keyed in Pierce's number to request doing the interview another time. As I was about to press send, my stomach quivered. I tossed the phone onto the seat, jumped out of the car and vomited at the curb.

Feeling better, I got back in my car, wiped my mouth with paper towels and decided I could do the interview after all. Moments after driving away, I saw about thirty white people, including young children, picking up trash along the sidewalks and on easements and putting the trash into plastic bags. I recalled from a TV report that they were members of a Unitarian church who volunteered one day a week to perform "cleanup" in The Gut Bucket.

Seconds later, I was forced to hit my brakes as two thugs, their ladies snuggled next to them, sat in their cars police-style blocking traffic in both directions, daring me and others to blow our horns or yell. Held hostage by those bastards, we waited. After ten minutes or so, they fist-bumped and crept away, grinning, Tupac thumping.

I drove on. Professionally made signs reading "Save Our Youth" stood in many yards only to be mocked by crude displays of dolls, basketballs and footballs, candles, crosses, plastic flowers and other items honoring murdered children.

At a four-way stop, a group of drug dealers milling under a banyan tree stared at my car, at my face and at my license plate. They were committing to memory everything about me, deciding if I was a potential customer, a harmless motorist or a "dead nigger driving," The Gut Bucket's name for a snitch in a vehicle. In my rearview mirror, I saw them passing final judgment, waving their arms at me dismissively.

They were *lords*, the only creatures enjoying impunity in The Gut Bucket.

Observing them in my mirror, I recalled a long-ago assignment I had at a farm that specialized in goat meat. My guide, an old watery-eyed Jamaican, and I approached a pen that held animals waiting to be slaughtered. He pointed to the dung heap in the pen. On top of the heap, two bucks fought for dominance, butting, twisting, pushing and bleating.

"Look at them two fools," the man said. "They gonna be chops and racks and flanks in thirty minutes, but they fighting to rule that pile a shit. Look at 'em. Ain't 'bout nothin'. Just like niggas in the 'hood."

I was thinking of those bucks as the Black Diaspora Museum came into view, six blocks from where I encountered the drug dealers. Mrs. Ella Pierce, the director, met me at the main entrance. A regal redbone, she spoke in a melodious contralto. I thought she would be taller and was disappointed that I had to look down at her.

The office was a tribute to civil rights, with memorabilia dating back to Reconstruction and thousands of scholarly books on floor-to-ceiling shelves. She sat at her desk, I in the leather chair in front of her.

Although we were aware of each other's reputations, that was our first in-person meeting, and we instantly disliked each other. Her features deadened as she evaluated me, a jigaboo who dared to pose as her equal. Our divide was the widest of all in Black life: pedigree. Born into the mulatto upper class, she had been spared the presence of a dark-skinned "common nigger" like me, the son of a long-haul truck driver and a hospital food service attendant.

"So, I finally meet Ron Clary, the infamous

columnist," she said, faking a smile as she peered over designer eyeglasses.

"I'm certain you mean famous, not infamous, Mrs. Pierce. A lot of people, even the well-born and highly educated like yourself, often make that mistake."

The enmity between us was beyond repair, so I turned on my recorder and addressed the reason for the interview: to gather material for a column about the new memorial to Jefferson Mims, the Black man who was shot at least twenty times and hanged by a white mob in 1902.

"You must be excited about the memorial," I said.

She leaned back and made a tent of her fingers. "I'm honored to unveil the memorial, which I'll perform in three weeks. It will remind people of the evil white people have perpetrated against us throughout history and what they still owe us."

"Is historical memory the same for white people as it is for Black people?"

"I don't understand the question," she said, fighting to control a sneer.

"Do you realistically think white people care about a plaque recognizing a Black man, a fruit picker, who was hanged and shot at least twenty times on Anise Boulevard more than a century ago?"

"Will this be the focus of your column?"

"No," I said, sensing her rising contempt. "Do you know that a Black man was murdered by another Black man this morning a few blocks from your memorial?"

"Your point?"

"My point? We spend too much time erecting memorials and painting murals on buildings, as if these things give us meaning. White people don't care about our memorials and murals. And based on what I see every day, most Black people right here in The Gut Bucket don't care either."

I was glad a knock came at the door, which opened,

and a young Black woman peeked in. Mrs. Pierce nodded to her.

"Doris Myers from Channel 4's in the lobby," the young woman said.

Mrs. Pierce looked at her watch. "My goodness! Tell her I'll be with her shortly."

The young woman smiled and left, and Mrs. Pierce turned back to me.

"Doris, your colleague, is always positive when she features us on her show."

Against my better judgment, I took the bait.

"That's because she's a white girl born and bred on an all-white, leafy boulevard in Silver Spring, Maryland," I said. "She's never lived in a Black ghetto with thieves, drug dealers and murderers.... Do you live here in The Gut Bucket?"

"It's Cedar Gardens, Mr. Clary. And, no, I don't live here. I live on Gumbo-Limbo Isle, and you know it. I'm quickly learning that you don't ask questions you don't have *your* answers to. Now, what's your point?"

Gumbo-Limbo Isle, nicknamed The Moat, was a wealthy enclave that tolerated a handful of prominent Blacks. Its two bridges posted armed guards.

"Isn't Commissioner Karl Murray one of your neighbors, and don't you attend his church?"

"Your point?"

"I don't know of any Black political or cultural or religious leaders who live in Cedar Gardens. Why's that?"

"You tell me."

"You won't like my verdict."

"Try me."

"Let's just drop it."

She smiled mischievously and said: "So, where does Mr. Ronald Clary live? Certainly not in Cedar Gardens."

"I lease an apartment in Heron Estates."

"Where do you worship?"

"The Atlantic Ocean, the Florida Straits, the Caribbean Sea and the Gulf of Mexico. The Pacific Ocean is a bit too far away, but I'd love to worship there."

"You're not a God-fearing Black man."

"I can't be afraid of what doesn't exist."

"So, the rumor's true: You're a Black atheist."

"Sounds like being Black really ups the ante."

"Do you pray?"

"You're upping the ante again."

"Do you ever pray, Mr. Clary?"

I restrained myself. "Could we get back to the memorial?"

"Please," she said, exasperated.

"Do you really believe all these monuments, murals and names on buildings and streets and parks will stop Black-on-Black carnage?"

"Turn it off," she said, pointing at my phone and

standing. "You give our enemies ammunition to keep us enslaved."

"We keep ourselves enslaved. I learned about the systemic horrors of racism and colorism as a child. We are condemned at conception, and too many of us let victimhood rot our brains and destroy the will to help ourselves."

"You can doubletalk and dress it up any way you want, but you're letting white people off the hook by blaming the victim, your own people."

"I'm as much a victim of racism as the drug dealers across the street. The difference between them and me is that I refuse to live as a victim. I'm self-aware enough to know that I have responsibilities for my own well-being. We can't change white people. We have to change ourselves. We're on our own. Even God doesn't want us. Life as a Black, especially in places like The Gut Bucket, is dehumanizing and hopeless if we let it be. I have a hard luck story, too, but it's not my whole life. I won't let it be."

She groaned. "People call you a self-loathing Uncle Tom. From what I heard today, you're the worst kind of self-loathing Uncle Tom. Do you want to know why, Mr. Clary?"

"Tell me."

"Because you have a soapbox. That white mullet wrapper."

"Mrs. Pierce, you obviously don't know the meaning of self-loathing," I said, realizing that I was committing a journalism no-no: attacking my subject.

"Please educate me," she said, scowling.

"Black-on-Black crime is self-loathing at its worst. Self-loathers brutalize their own people. I've never robbed a Black person; never sold drugs to a Black child; never impregnated a Black woman and abandoned her; never urinated or defecated in a Black person's yard. And although I've wanted to kill a few thugs over the years, I've never killed or injured a

Black person." I paused to gauge her anger before continuing. "I wrote about the slaughter of eight-year-old Tiana Mitchell. Remember her?"

"Well, of course."

"That child was asleep in bed hugging her doll, *Sweetie Pooh*. Twenty bullets shredded her little body. The Canal Dawgs and the Mangrove E-Lights were fighting over some nigger mess in front of Tiana's house. And what did we do? We put that dead child's name on a street sign. No one's gone to the police. Naming that street for Tiana is a travesty of everything decent. Her killers are still out here, down the street. And you and these so-called leaders remain silent. That's self-loathing."

Her nostrils flared. "I wrote the proclamation to name that street to honor Tiana."

"I know you wrote it, and I'm telling you that the only way to honor Tiana is to make compost out of the animals who killed her. Unless, of course, you think building Tiana a memorial is better than taking her killers off the street. Actually, we could do both: Take the killers off the street and build a memorial for the child."

"I've never heard a Black person talk so crazy like this."

"Like this? Like what? The truth is that we keep ourselves down by acting out white people's ugly expectations of us. When they drive through The Gut Bucket and see our violence and filth and indolence, it only hardens their hatred. I just saw a group of white people picking up trash down the street from here. Why must white people pick up our trash in our neighborhood?"

"To ease their conscience."

"No, it's an indictment of us. Doesn't that bother you?"

"When is this write-up running?" she said, folding her arms.

"I'll let you know."

"Don't think I want to read it."

I gathered my belongings, she opened the door and I walked out. As I neared the lobby, Doris Myers, white and attractive, came straight at me and stopped in my path. Her videographer, a pretty young Black woman I had seen from a distance once, stood beside her.

"Ron, I always say your photo in that paper is a disservice to you," Doris said, looking me up and down, then turning to the videographer and winking. "I've been trying to molest him for five years, and I'm beginning to suspect that he's a virgin or some kind of queer. Off the record, Ron, which is it, virgin or some kind of queer or all of the above?"

The videographer chuckled, covering her mouth with her hand.

"Hello, Doris," I said, trying to maintain a straight face. I liked her sense of humor.

"I won't forgive you if you left Mrs. Pierce pissed off," she said. "We're taping my interview with her for tomorrow night's show about the Jefferson Mims Memorial."

"The doyenne's fired up and ready to go."

"Meaning you pissed her off."

"Good ear."

"A job requirement. Don't miss my show. Eight o'clock."

I seldom missed her show, but I dared not massage her ego by acknowledging it. The videographer gave me that side-to-side neck move, then prolonged stink eye. Doris grinned as I walked away.

Having met Mrs. Pierce, I realized that she was like so many other Blacks who saw themselves as Keepers of Negritude. While eager to disparage so-called "sellouts" like me, they withered when faced with logic and reason. Far too many of them considered being Black to be a noble calling and that Black suffering was a gift from God. I regularly heard Blacks say they were proud to be Black. Even as a child, I wondered why anyone would be proud to belong to the most despised group in the universe. It was lunacy to my young mind.

Disappointed with myself, I got into my car. How would I use the material I had collected? My intention had been to praise Mrs. Pierce as the stalwart leader who had conceived of the Jefferson Mims Memorial and had shepherded it to reality. But as I heard sirens and saw police and emergency vehicles racing by, I thought of the Black-on-Black atrocities that occurred each week without public expressions of outrage from the likes of Mrs. Pierce.

I could not write a puff piece about a leader whose silence amounted to complicity in crime and tragedy.

3

I drove to my favorite spot on the Atlantic Ocean, a stretch that had not succumbed to wealth and the machines of progress. Alone, I took off my shoes and socks, rolled up my pants and walked on the white sand that was hot and soft between my toes. Inhaling the salty air, I stepped into the swirling cool water and let it massage my feet and calves. The sensation reminded me of my childhood years in Sable Beach, when I walked and fished many days after school on the Atlantic shore, my escape from the ghetto, when even as a child I resented the cruel irony of living in stench and filth and violence while wealth, beauty and other amenities of the beachfront beckoned only a few miles away.

I always was aware of the deficits in Black life: the inbred backwardness, the self-destruction, the disrespectfulness, the religiosity and the violence. My awareness of those deficits inspired me to defy expectations that I, "a ghetto nigger," would "amount to nothing." I was determined to transcend that. I would "amount to something," but on my own terms, by my own definition. As a result, Black adults labeled me a "rebellious, nappy-headed little nigger."

And I recalled the many weekends when a few of my buddies and I would go crabbing on Jamaica River along Cormorant Terrace in downtown. We loved bringing our catches home to our families. Often, as I held a chicken neck on a line as bait, I lapsed into daydreams and forgot about crabbing, instead focusing on the yachts and beautiful people aboard them. I was captivated by the scantily clad women who sunbathed on the decks, painted their nails, sipped tall colorful drinks and read books and magazines.

The only Blacks, women and men, I ever saw on those yachts wore uniforms. They mopped decks and polished railings, ran errands, babysat and walked dogs whose shit they had to discard. Even as a child, I could see their *damned* expressions, the defeat in their motions, their demoralized way of staring skyward, never relaxing and enjoying paradise. Watching them, I vowed to avoid such humiliation. Of course, I dreamed of owning a yacht and sailing with beautiful women to exotic places.

Thinking about the dead Haitian in that dusty parking lot, I felt those same childhood deficits as I watched a cruise ship head out to sea and as an osprey cried and hovered over the water. The bird descended, spread its talons, hit the surface of the water and rose with a sea bass. Struggling briefly in that jittery way, the osprey adjusted its grip and flew to a nest atop an Australian pine about thirty yards away. Little heads popped up in the nest as the adult approached.

About three hours of daylight remained. Ordinarily, I would have stayed to watch sunset and toss in a fishing line to catch dinner. But on that afternoon, I felt compelled to return to The Gut Bucket.

When I neared the mall, about three hundred boisterous onlookers milled around the parking lot behind police crime tape. I turned on my video as a shirtless thug ripped down a section of the tape. A Black cop strolled over and stood where the tape had been removed, his hand on his weapon.

"Stay back," he said. "This is still an active crime scene."

"Fuck you!" someone yelled.

The cop did not react. The Haitian's body had been removed, and blood, black and purple, had congealed on the ground. Flies swarmed on the spot, and a superior officer signaled for the patrolman to remove the tape.

Young dudes, their tattooed arms folded, spoke in their codes as detectives tried to gather information. A boom box played a Nipsey Hussle rap, and dozens of shirtless teens circled the parking lot on freestyle bicycles. One bumped into a girl, no more than seventeen or eighteen, who was carrying an infant in her arm and pulling a wailing toddler alongside.

Two large hand-scrawled signs had been raised behind the parking lot. One read, "Snitches Get Stitches." The other read, "Snitches Get Ditches." Hennessy cognac, knotty head gin and Colt 45 malt liquor flowed freely, and the odor of marijuana filled the air.

I was witnessing a carnival where an innocent man had been murdered a few hours earlier. Young children frolicked, and many thugs wore R.I.P. T-shirts bearing images of their dead comrades.

One of the hundreds of crazy men in The Gut Bucket shadowboxed at the intersection. A street preacher, wearing a dirty white sheet as his cassock, bayed at the sky, his tattered Bible held high over his head. A young hooker strutted past, performed a fuck-gyration for the preacher's benefit and pranced away, the preacher's eyes following her.

As the sun went down, the lot became a party scene. A local rap group entertained, accompanied by scantily clad female dancers. The performances were excellent, and I was certain the group would become rich and famous if they escaped The Gut Bucket's violence.

4

I did not go to the newsroom as was my routine but instead drove to my apartment, poured a glass of Jack Daniels, sat on my patio and watched fishing boats return for the day with their catches. A Royal Caribbean cruise ship headed to some exotic destination, and I imagined being on that voyage, never seeing The Gut Bucket again.

Watching pelicans glide over the channel in a chevron formation, I recalled that most of the witnesses to the killing filmed everything and took selfies. For some, the selfies would be a curio. For others, the images would bring instant street cred and give them entry into a shadow world that protected its own from *whitey*.

After showering, I went into my office, turned on the video and became sick as I watched the Haitian clutch his stomach, fall to his knees, collapse, reach out and utter *that* name. I studied the faces of the witnesses and saw enjoyment. I watched the video again and took notes. The people's behavior was inapprehensible, and one section of the action stopped me cold. It was of church ladies in various stages of their coiffures hurrying out of Blessed Life Beauty Salon to observe. Their faces, like all the others there, were animated with anticipation of a bloody spectacle.

I turned off the video, switched on the TV and caught the end of a news report on the murder. A white female reporter said: "According to police spokesman Lyle Turner, no witnesses have come forward in today's shooting death of local building contractor and Haitian community leader Emile Pomet."

Turner, a Black man in his early fifties, appeared on the screen. "We know a crowd was present before, during and after Mr. Pomet was shot," he said. "Many people know who killed this gentleman. If we had one witness to come forward, that would be a great start in solving this tragedy. We know that dozens of people, maybe a hundred, have stills and videos of the shooting. Too bad there aren't any surveillance cameras on the buildings. Once again, this no-snitch subculture is hindering our work and letting another murderer, or murderers, freely walk the streets."

The reporter reappeared and said that Emile Pomet was part of a group of Haitians who had established successful businesses in Mangrove Shores after "leaving their island nation's bloodletting and natural disasters." He had been president of the Haitian Commerce Association and was set to become a U.S. citizen during the next swearing in ceremony at City Hall.

I had two more fingers of Jack Daniels and went to bed, falling asleep thinking about Emile and the many witnesses to the killing, including myself.

At five the next morning, I went outside for the paper. The murder, with a recent photo of Emile at a construction site, was the lead story. After reading, I showered, dressed and ate wheat toast and yogurt for breakfast, not enjoying it. Before going to the newspaper office, I phoned a Black cop, a lieutenant, I had known since my police beat days and asked him if anyone had identified Emile's killer.

"Fuck no," he said.

"Let me know if someone does."

"Don't hold your breath," he said contemptuously. "In my sixteen years on the force, never had a snitch – a good Black citizen. Not one. Killers walking the streets in broad daylight."

I drove to the newspaper and found a note from Asa Sterling on my desk asking me to come to his office. Asa was the paper's first Black opinions editor, and I liked working for him because he left me alone, and I liked drinking bourbon and fishing with him on his cabin cruiser. Sitting next to his desk, I found him as ruminative as ever.

He handed me copies of three building construction magazines.

"Great articles about Emile Pomet in these, the man shot down yesterday in The Bucket," he said. "I want you to do a column about him. He was my friend, so I can't write it. Give me one of your two-thousand-word navel gazers. You spent over a year in Haiti on assignment and vacationed there, so you're familiar with the culture. That capacious memory of yours should come in handy."

"Since when did you start giving me assignments?"

"As we speak," he said, striking his often-used pose of philosophical meditation.

"How did you know Emile?"

"His company built my lanai and put in my swimming pool. Excellent work. I recommended him to a lot of other people. His wife, Alphonsine, will be your major source. She teaches art at the university, and she's a docent at Prentice Art Museum." He sighed and rubbed his beard. "The police probably won't find his killer or killers. These niggers won't talk. As Zora Neale Hurston used to say, 'My people. My people.'"

Asa was talking to one of Zora's people. I had not gone to the police, either. He frowned at my long hesitation.

"Something wrong?"

"Nah, just thinking," I said, reliving the shooting and searching for a suitable reply to the most principled journalist I knew.

If I had told him I witnessed Emile's murder and filmed it, he would have insisted on my going to the police. And, of course, I could not write anything about Emile. Worse, I thought he would have fired me. I did not understand my own reasoning at the time, so I said nothing. I was not prepared to go to the police and as a journalist, I was intrigued by the silence of the witnesses.

Asa cleared his throat.

"Are you still writing Sunday's column about the Jefferson Mims Memorial and Mrs. Pierce?"

"No. Giving you an evergreen about pollution in Canal Park."

"Nothing like an evergreen about pollution with a cup of coffee on Sunday morning," he said, enjoying his own humor. "I guess you know Mrs. Pierce phoned demanding I fire you. If I don't, she's going to the old curmudgeon upstairs who pays our 'filthy lucre,' as she calls it."

"The Race Woman doesn't think much of the Fourth Estate, eh?"

"No shit."

We laughed.

"Are you going to fire me?"

"Not before you write the Emile piece," he said.

"Giselle and I are having a party at our place Saturday night. Beautiful women from her office will be there. We want you to come, so don't give me a pile of bullshit."

"No bullshit. I have plans."

He did not believe me, but he shook his head and let it go.

5

I returned to The Gut Bucket in my pickup because I had driven my car the day before. I parked three blocks from the mall. Wearing faded jeans, an old fishing shirt, scruffy dock siders and dark eyeglasses, I trudged along the sidewalk trying to blend in.

Everything felt wrong when I neared four impeccably dressed Black Muslims selling *The Final Call*, the Nation of Islam's weekly tabloid. What am I doing here? I wondered. Just give the video of the killing to the police anonymously. Dreadlocks would be arrested, and it would be out of my hands whether or not he was convicted. I would have performed my duty as a law-abiding citizen.

That grand notion faded as I watched witnesses milling about. I knew I would not send the video to the police anytime soon because I wanted to see what would transpire during the next few weeks. How would the witnesses treat the cold-blooded public killing of an innocent man?

I decided to interview five witnesses, a manageable number, to learn if they were or were not going to the police and why.

Keeping my face down, I strolled along the sidewalk. The parking lot had its usual ingathering of thugs, whores and old men playing cards and dominoes under the canopies. Not knowing what to expect, I entered Cue Man for the first time ever and was surprised that it was well-lit and clean.

Rap music thumped and the barkeep nodded to me as I walked to him. No one whispered or eyeballed me as I sat at the bar, which meant that I was not considered a threat.

"Help you, brother?" Barkeep said.

I ordered two fingers of Jim Beam and turned toward the four busy pool tables where all of the players, dressed in sagging, little-boy outfits, were talking shit and guffawing. The odor of marijuana suffused the air, and I knew I would get a buzz if I stayed much longer.

Dreadlocks, accompanied by a giant thug, sauntered in from a side room, a joint between his thumb and forefinger. Gold chains hung around his neck, and he sported an expensive wristwatch and diamond rings. His handsome face carried reckless authority. He was someone you "didn't fuck with," a grotesque peacock with a groveling entourage.

"S'up? S'up?" he said, slapping hands with many in the room, including me.

I just slapped hands with a murderer, I thought.

Years of reporting and living in ghettos had taught me that being an exemplary thug, a survivor, meant knowing the ethos, the way of life, performing outside the law while thriving in plain sight. A cop I interviewed in Liberty City following a gang-related massacre told me that thugs want people to know they are "bad motherfuckers, and they want people to know that they know they are bad motherfuckers." It was not just fear that held people's tongues. It also was the pride that came with dedicated silence, belonging to a family, keeping dangerous secrets – even self-destructive ones – and defying the white man's crusade to destroy you.

And there I was in the presence of Dreadlocks, a preening bastard who did not read the newspaper. He nodded to Barkeep for a drink. I was nothing more than a speck on The Gut Bucket wallpaper, which was fine with me because it meant I was safe until I became known.

While anonymity was part of my plan, I also knew that ghetto dwellers were some of the most perceptive people anywhere. At critical moments, they instinctively smelled alien threats, especially the threat of what I once heard a thug describe as "the funk of an Uncle Tom." They always looked for signs of the press: notebooks, recorders, intense eyeballing and cameras.

Because I had witnessed Emile's killing, I was cautious and assessed my chances of escaping through one of two doors or through one of three windows if it came to that. One of my recurring nightmares was being killed by a worthless Gut Bucket thug.

Almost everyone gathered around Dreadlocks. Even the wagering players lowered their cue sticks to listen to his prattle about "the fine new 'hos at the university." Barkeep, who had witnessed the killing, rushed to him with a bottle of Colt 45 malt liquor, and I moved from the bar to the darkest corner of the room between the cue stick rack and the toilet.

Dressed in matching camouflage cargoes, black T-shirts and untied boots, Hoodie and Rasta entered through the back door and slapped hands with Dreadlocks. Hoodie wore Emile's watch, proudly displaying it.

Dreadlocks looked at the wall clock. "Got to hook up with my Nubian queen. Later, you sorry-ass niggers."

A scruffy OG, who had witnessed Emile's murder, swirled on his barstool and addressed Dreadlocks: "They say that *new bean queen* got yo' ass pussy-whupped, fool boy."

"Nubian, dumb-ass old nigger," Dreadlocks yelled as if to a deaf mute. "Nubian, motherfucker! Nubian!"

The room burst into laughter. Dreadlocks grinned, slapped hands around the room and sauntered out the back door, Giant Thug following. Hoodie and Rasta grabbed cue sticks. I went out the front door, walked to the side of the building and saw Dreadlocks and Giant Thug carousing with two drug dealers I recognized. I trotted to my truck, and Dreadlocks stayed with the men a few more minutes before walking to a mint-condition 1959 Chevy Impala convertible lowrider. He got in and drove away, rap lyrics blasting. Giant Thug reentered Cue Man.

I followed Dreadlocks. After several blocks, he turned into the circular drive of an expensive house with a two-car garage and manicured lawn. The home was luxurious, out of place in The Gut Bucket, which meant that he was the hustler's hustler. No one dared to "fuck with" him. He parked in the drive behind a BMW M4, and I parked a block away under an oak just as he sprang from the car, trotted to the house and used his key to let himself in.

A few minutes later, he and an attractive Black woman emerged. I assumed she was the Nubian queen who had "pussy-whupped" him.

He wheeled a large cooler, and she carried a picnic bag. They put everything in the lowrider and drove away, bone-shaking rap playing, their heads bobbing and their bodies moving in sync. I followed them to a Bayfront park where they met three other Black couples at a pavilion. I parked behind a thicket of sea grape and palmetto. That time of day, we had the area to ourselves.

While Dreadlocks lit the barbecue grill, the others partied. Then, the group, including Dreadlocks, trotted to the shoreline and frolicked in the shallows. After the charcoal was ready, they grilled burgers and steaks, and they partied for about three hours, eating, drinking, smoking pot and dancing to rap on a boom box.

They had all the appearance of being normal people enjoying themselves on our famous waterfront. Before sunset, they drove back to the house and entered. I parked out of view as Hoodie and Rasta arrived with their dates.

Having seen enough of them for one day, I drove home, grabbed the newspaper, poured a healthy Jack Daniels and walked onto the porch. The lead story was not about Emile but about the fatal shooting of a rapper and three of his band members the previous

night at a concert in The Gut Bucket, which I had not

heard about.

I moved down the page below the fold to get away

from ugly stories about Blacks. No such luck. The

first headline read: "Emile Pomet left a rich legacy."

The story carried a photo of Emile and one of his

forty-one-year-old widow, Professor Alphonsine

Beauvais Pomet. Although the article discussed

Emile's business acumen and philanthropy, it

lavished praise on his wife, the art history professor

and painter. In the photos, Alphonsine, a Henri de

Toulouse-Lautrec scholar, was beautiful and dark-

skinned. The lead photo was of her in her office.

Thin, curvaceous and tall, she wore a dark blazer and

multi-colored pants. Toulouse-Lautrec's paintings

hung around the office.

Looking at her photo, I knew she was why Emile

had struggled to live, reaching out for her,

muttering her name, wanting to remain alive to be with her.

One tidbit, in the sidebar, was that Emile was "an aficionado of haute horology." Unfamiliar with the term, I looked it up: "Haute horology refers to the absolute finest of high watchmaking." That explained the watch he wore when he was murdered. I had not cried since my parents died, but I was close to crying as I tossed the paper onto the table. Hoodie had stolen a dead man's beloved possession. I felt an anger I rarely felt.

6

Next morning, I drove to the university to meet Professor Alphonsine Beauvais Pomet. A student pointed me to the art department, and I found the professor's name on the first-floor directory. I reminded myself that I was acting unprofessionally because I always arranged my interviews to avoid ugly surprises, unless ugly surprise was my plan.

I dreaded meeting the woman whose husband I had seen murdered, and since I did not have prepared questions, I felt like a voyeur and did not know what I would say to her. At her office, I looked through the glass partition wall and was glad she was not there. On the desk were manila folders, several books, two decorative teacups, a business card holder and photos of the professor and Emile and what I assumed to be photos of their parents and siblings. The walls held prints of Haitian, African and French art.

"May I be of assistance?" a woman's lilting voice asked behind me. I heard Creole in the accent and knew she was not of the Haitian upper class.

I turned and looked into the eyes of Professor Alphonsine Beauvais Pomet, Emile Pomet's widow. She was taller than she appeared in the newspaper photo, and while that photo had captured her beauty and sultriness, the face of the woman in front of me was one of anguish.

"Professor Pomet?" I said.

"Monsieur Clary."

I was surprised. "You know who I am."

"Emile and I often thought of calling you to discuss some of the knotty issues you raised."

"I apologize for coming unannounced."

"It's part of your job description, to get the scoop, as you all call it," she said, her tone dolorous. "I know many other journalists."

After she moved past me and opened the door, I felt

the gross insensitivity of my being there so soon after her husband's death. Moving gracefully, she wore the same kind of unassuming attire in the newspaper photo. I followed her, and she waved for me to sit in the chair beside the desk. She sat behind the desk, her silhouette framed in morning sunlight.

"Professor Pomet, my editor asked me to write a column about your husband."

"Please call me Alphonsine."

"I'm Ron."

"Is Ron your Christian name?"

"Ronald."

"A fine name. It means 'mighty counselor' or 'ruler.'"

"Thanks for telling me."

"I know because of Ronald Rae's sculptures. I wrote a paper on him for a conference several years ago."

"Sorry. Never heard of him."

She started to speak but stopped to dab at her eyes with a tissue.

"He's Scottish," she said, her voice unsteady. "All of his works are in hand-carved granite…. My favorite is *Widow Woman*. Emile and I saw it in the U.K."

A cruel irony, I thought.

"Forgive me for coming unannounced," I said. "Maybe we can talk another time."

"Yes, in a few days."

We exchanged business cards and we stood.

"I'll email you," I said.

"Ekselan."

I let myself out, and as I walked past the window wall, I saw her opening a book of prints and dabbing at her eyes. I wanted to return and comfort her.

At home, I changed into old jeans, a rumpled fishing shirt, a floppy hat and dark sunglasses. I drove to the Mall of African Peoples and parked in the alley behind the parking lot. With a view of the entire area, I played my video of the murder and studied witnesses.

An hour later, Dreadlocks, accompanied by Rasta, drove the lowrider into the lot and parked in his designated spot. They got out, swaggered into the building but quickly came out and got back into the car. I followed them to the community garden, which I had written about, where about fifty men of various ages sat in old metal chairs and on milk crates playing cards and dominoes. Others stood around under the trees talking and checking out passersby. The neglected garden, envisioned to great fanfare as a food lifeline for the poor, had mostly dying and dead plants.

Dreadlocks and Rasta hopped from the car and strutted to four men playing blackjack at a table made of saw horses and plywood. Dreadlocks went to Giant Thug, who was wearing a wife beater, a crocheted beanie and camouflage cargo trousers. They bumped elbows, and Giant Thug whispered to Dreadlocks. They laughed.

A police cruiser passed without braking. No one seemed to notice, and the two cops did not turn their heads. I studied the faces scattered around the garden and recognized several witnesses to Emile's murder.

Dreadlocks walked to his car several times with different men, Giant Thug watching. After the men got in the car, Dreadlocks handed them drugs, they paid, exited the car and went their separate ways. Dreadlocks returned to the table and waited for his next customers.

I left the area before my anonymity ran out. Remembering that I needed food in my apartment, I drove to my regular grocery store and while checking out, I saw Dreadlocks' Nubian Queen working at the customer service counter. So, this is where I remember you from, I thought, pushing my cart.

To learn more about her, I went to the lottery

station, filled out a ticket and got in line. Her name,

Imani Barrett, and her photo were on the wall with

those of others in that department. She was the

customer care manager.

"May I help you, sir?" she asked.

Given her professionalism and attractiveness, I

could not believe that she was Dreadlock's woman,

the lover of a cold-blooded killer. As I paid for my

ticket, I saw her gold engagement ring. I left the store,

got in my pickup, drove to where I could see the

employee parking area and waited, assuming that

Imani's shift ended at five.

At five-fifteen, she exited the store and got in the

BMW that had been parked at the house in The Gut

Bucket. I followed her, allowing a lot of distance.

She pulled onto the campus of a private elementary

school in a white neighborhood several miles from

The Gut Bucket. I parked under a banyan tree across

the street while she inched forward in a long line of other vehicles in the student pick-up area. A pretty brown-skinned girl, perhaps eight years old, skipped from the building, waving happily, and came to Imani, who had gotten out of the BMW. She took the child's book bag, hugged and kissed her and helped her into the car.

They drove to a nearby McDonald's, bought two slushies in the drive-thru and drove to Dreadlocks' house. They parked and went inside. Watching the door shut behind them, I wondered if Imani Barrett knew that her fiancé, who I assumed was the girl's father, had murdered an unarmed man. Would it matter if she knew?

7

After putting away my groceries, I studied witnesses of the murder on my video. Having become familiar with many faces, I drove to the Mall of African Peoples and parked in the alley behind the basketball court. Darkness was falling and the usual crowd had amassed. Hoodie and Rasta played basketball, each showing exceptional skills. Hip-hop blasted and the odor of pot floated in the hot air.

Watching the duo play, I decided not to interview them because I knew they would cool pose and talk shit in that thug monotone that I detested. My next thought was unsettling: These two boys – and they were boys despite their self-delusions about manhood – were the future of The Gut Bucket.

Why am I here tonight? I thought.

Looking at the crowd, I knew I was trying to quell my sense of complicity in Emile's killing, trying to convince myself, again, that I was being the journalist, the objective observer collecting material for a column that could make a positive difference.

The big questions were clear: Why had no one gone to the police? Who would be the first? Would I be the lone snitch? Could I and some others have stopped Dreadlocks from firing that Glock?

I walked to where Emile had taken his last breath. Black dirt from the alley had been spread over the spot and the surrounding area. I turned and saw Hoodie and Rasta slapping hands, their team having destroyed the opponent.

"You niggas shoot like bitches and 'hos!" Hoodie yelled.

The crowd cracked up.

"One hundred big ones," Rasta said, holding out his hand.

A member of the losing team handed Hoodie two fifties. I wondered if any of those young thugs had experienced a moment of innocent childhood or if they had oozed from the womb precocial, walking, talking, gangbanging and murdering.

When my phone vibrated in my pocket, I walked away from the basketball court and saw that it was Alphonsine. I answered with trepidation: "Hello."

"Ronald, I'm glad to speak with you. Matters are changing by the moment. I'm flying to Miami tomorrow morning, then to Haiti on Friday. You're welcome to come to my home for the interview after I return from Haiti. I'll telephone you."

She gave me her address on Pelican Bayou, an exclusive isle near downtown where home prices started at three million. I knew that a few Blacks lived there, but I did not know one personally.

"Thank you," I said, admiring her calm under the circumstances.

Hanging up, I inhaled the distinct aroma of fish and walked to where an old woman was ladling fried sheepshead out of a cast iron wash pot and placing the fish on a well-used Dutch platter. She looked up at me and smiled, her front teeth missing.

"Best sheepshead in The Bucket," she said.

"A sandwich with plenty of hot sauce and mustard," I said.

As she made my sandwich, I realized that she was on my video, but I decided that because of her age and frailty, I would not interview her. I paid her and ate the delicious sheepshead as I walked back to the basketball court.

Rasta and Hoodie stood on the sideline flirting with two girls. The four of them walked to a table where a man sold hand-churned ice cream. They ordered cones and ate like *normal* teens.

I walked around the lot for another hour. Next to where Emile died, an impromptu Crip walk challenge had started, rap music thumping from a monster boom box. Contestants danced with creative moves and the crowd celebrated. Bets were made, and the odor of marijuana settled in the air.

At home, I went online and Googled Emile Pomet. The hundreds of entries, particularly international ones, surprised me. I spent the next three days reading, taking notes, conducting phone interviews and exchanging emails with builders and architects who had worked with Emile. Even as a cynical journalist, I was surprised that no one spoke negatively of Emile. On the morning of the fourth day, I telephoned my cop contact, and he said no witnesses to the murder had come forward.

Moments after we hung up, Alphonsine telephoned.

"Hello and welcome back," I said.

"Mesi. I hope you've been well during my absence. As I said before, you may come to my home for the interview. Does noon tomorrow suit you?"

"Yes."

"Esplandid. I'll have lunch prepared. Any

prohibitions?"

"No lion fish," I said, trying to be lighthearted.

"In the hands of the right chef, it's safe and delectable."

"Should I bring anything?"

"Just your notebook and phone. No camera."

We said goodbye. I spent the rest of the day writing questions for the interview and reading about Henri de Toulouse-Lautrec, remembering that my professors at Columbia had taught us that important, busy people respected well-informed journalists and enjoyed talking with them.

Next afternoon, I drove to Alphonsine's home. Moments after I rang the bell, the door opened, and she was smiling bravely, her shapely form outlined beneath a simple floral dress.

"Bonjou, Ronald."

"Thanks, professor."

"I insist that you address me as Alphonsine now

that you've crossed my threshold."

"Alphonsine."

I followed her from the alcove toward a sunny room with an expansive view of the bayou. Along the way, there were dozens of famous works of art, original paintings and prints and sculptures. The large print beside the east window of the living room pulled me in.

"Walker Sickert's *Mornington Crescent Nude*," I said, glad to see something I recognized to show her that I, an American ghetto Black, had at least one redeeming trait.

"How did you learn about Sickert, Ronald?"

"Courtauld Gallery in London when I was an exchange student. I fell in love with his work, especially this one."

"Why this one in particular?"

"It's ethereal and yet realistically sexy," I said trying not to sound phony.

"I would give an A-plus for that pithy answer if you were my student."

"When did you see your first Sickert?"

"Emile introduced me to his work on our first trip to London."

She led me to a huge bamboo rocker facing a stand of black mangrove. I sat and the chair's sheer size reminded me of a Dali, and I felt like a character in one of his paintings.

"Relax while I prepare tea," she said, handing me a book, *Toulouse-Lautrec and the Fin de Siecle*, by David Sweetman. "One of my required texts. Fortunately, my students love it. Excuse me for a few minutes."

As I thumbed through the beautiful book, she returned with two cups of tropical green tea and placed them on the table between the rocking chairs. The aroma transported me back to my childhood in Sable Beach, reminding me of the wild guavas we used to pick in back yards and alleys and abandoned lots. She noticed when I looked in the direction of the kitchen and inhaled.

"We're having lambi Creole, which is conch cooked in a spicy sauce. Everything is prepared. Just warming."

I did not tell her that I had the dish often when I was in Port-au-Prince.

"Beautiful aroma," I said.

"Are you married, Ronald?"

"Haven't met the right woman."

"You must be hopelessly discriminating or an incurable grouch. How unhappy I would've been if my Emile had been like you."

"You both were fortunate."

"I was a little tart when Emile met me."

The word "tart" was surprising coming from her.

"How's your tea?" she asked.

"Delicious. I must ask about your 'little tart'

comment."

"Indeed," she said, looking at a brown pelican dive. "I was a child of sixteen when Emile found me on a street in Port-au-Prince. He was carousing with colleagues, and I was trying to find American tourists to give me U.S. dollars. No, I wasn't a prostitute. My family needed to pay the rent, and being cute and thin, I could easily collect money from men by putting on a sweet face while I begged. It was dehumanizing but I did it.

"Emile and his group were strolling past when he looked into my eyes and asked me my name. I told him and he said it was beautiful. He was so handsome, the very picture of Haiti's elite, and I was of the dark-skinned lower caste. He inquired of my age and school and home address. He scolded me for being a common beggar. I was mortified. He led me to a shiny Mercedes and seated me in front between himself and the driver. I was afraid because I thought they were going to rape and kill me. I felt abandoned by Papa Legba."

"Papa Legba?"

"In Haitian voodoo, Papa Legba is an intermediary between humans and the spirit world. Emile touched my arm after the car moved. His fingers were so reassuring. It was the first time I relaxed in the company of men. All men, young and old, always tried to bed me. I had no idea where Emile was taking me, but after several blocks, the truth became clear. He was taking me home, to our tin and plywood shack. When we arrived, I was ashamed. We got out, and he followed me along our dirt path. My mother opened the door and screamed his name.

"I was shocked that she knew this man who had brought me home so unceremoniously. He addressed my mother by her name, Esterline, even apologizing for visiting unannounced. Unbeknownst to me, my father was a laborer for Emile's building company.

Emile wanted to know why I was a common beggar on the street. Embarrassed, my mother explained that we struggled to live on my father's salary. Now, it was Emile's turn to be ashamed. He was not paying my father a living wage for his family, and he wanted to know how many souls we had in our household.

"We had seven souls. He asked my mother about my status in school. I was in vocational training to become a secretary, and my mother also said I was a gifted artist, a painter. Emile asked me if I wanted a job after school in his office. I said yes and my parents gave me permission. That, Ronald, is how I came to know Emile Lucian Pomet."

Listening to her, I relived Emile's murder, how Hoodie had kicked Emile and had taken his watch, how I, like others, had done nothing to help. She dabbed at tears with her hand and stood.

"Forgive me," she said and rushed from the room.

She returned with a box of tissues and placed it

within easy reach.

"Should I come back another time?" I asked.

"I'm fine now," she said, clearing her throat. "I haven't cried in many years…. Emile was ideal in every way. He never touched me intimately until we were married, a year after I graduated from high school. He invited me to dinner one night at his beautiful home. In his living room, he had a print of *The Black Countess* by Henri de Toulouse-Lautrec. I fell in love with that painting and with Toulouse-Lautrec. I wanted to be that countess, driving that beautiful horse on that French beach. Emile was amused. He said that's when he fell in love with me, and he asked me if I wanted to be his countess. It was a fantasy come true.

"He remembered that I painted and asked to see my work. That was the beginning of my real life in art. We went to Paris, leased a home and stayed there for several years, until I earned a doctorate in art history at Sorbonne University. Emile worked for a building construction firm. We returned to Port-au-Prince, and I became an art professor. Emile became heavily involved in liberal politics, and when matters became increasingly dangerous, we came to America. We tried Little Haiti, but it was insane and violent. We had friends in Mangrove Shores, so we moved here."

As I was about to speak, she glanced at the wall clock.

"Let's dine."

She seated me in the dining room, went to the kitchen and returned with our food and a bottle of Antinori Guado al Tasso. It was my best meal in months.

"You spent time in Haiti," she said refilling our wine glasses. "Emile and I read your excellent dispatches about restaveks and wondered why they interested you."

"In Sable Beach, I saw a lot of Haitian girls

working for rich Americans and Haitian expats. I got

to know a few of them and was so intrigued that I

went to Haiti to learn more about the restavek

custom."

"You know, of course, that it's actually indentured

servitude."

"Yes, as far as I understand it. I got a lot of

misdirection during interviews."

"That's the fate of most inquisitive outsiders," she

said, noticing how much I enjoyed the food. "I must

confess that I can't take credit for our lunch. My

Haitian maid prepared everything, and I gave her the

remainder of the day off. And no, Ronald, we didn't

drag a poor child from Haiti to be our slave. We

placed an ad in your newspaper, and it was answered

by Marie Louise, who's thirty-eight and married.

Emile was helping her open her own restaurant. He'd

found a wonderful property, and I'm going to make

sure it's financially sound before I leave."

"Permanently?"

"Yes. I'm taking Emile's cremains home, but I'll come back to complete the semester with my students. Then, I'm returning to the homeland."

"But why? Haiti's a...."

"A voodoo-ridden dystopia. We have cultivated a stoicism that saves us. We have a grim existence, and to survive we must face a world that's hostile to our very presence. It's the same for American Blacks, but most of you all aren't aware of your predicament. Sorry. In Haiti, voodoo can't get rid of the stoicism, the Catholic Church either. President Jean-Claude Duvalier said it best: It is the destiny of the people of Haiti to suffer. It's the same for Blacks in America. As grim as all that sounds, I rise each morning and face the day because I have no choice. Now, I *must* face my days without Emile. Come. Let's change the subject. I want to show you why I don't want you to take photos."

She led me into the house, down a hallway and opened a door. We stepped inside a large room, and she switched on a light. The room had many glass display cases strategically placed, each case containing rows of expensive watches.

"How many watches are here?"

"Timepieces," she said. "Emile would never say watches. How many? I don't know. If you name a company or brand, it's probably here. Eberhard, Baume & Mercier, Cartier, Rolex, Heuer, Bulova, Doxa, Cyma Longines, Vulcain…. I know many names from being in Emile's orbit. If you write about us, please don't mention the timepieces. Thieves would kill me and make off with them before I can transport them to Miami for valuation.

"I don't know what the collection is worth. Perhaps millions. Emile began collecting as a child – pawnshops, second-hand stores, family estate sales. Each one is catalogued in that computer in the corner, which is going to Miami. Timepieces didn't really interest me until now.

"When Emile died, he was wearing a rare one manufactured by the Movado Company in the 1920s. I know because I saw it on his arm when he left. The police said it wasn't on him when they recovered his body. He loved its craftsmanship. I'll never see it again. At least they returned our wedding ring."

I felt crushing guilt and briefly looked away. For the next two hours, we discussed Emile's work and his politics, and we finished the bottle of wine.

"The owner of that billiards room where Emile was killed asked Emile to renovate it," she said, staring at our empty glasses. "Shall I open another bottle?"

"No," I said, wanting more wine but too embarrassed to acknowledge it.

She nodded. "Emile had great plans for that billiards room. He wanted to make it a showcase for that part of town. Have you been to this place?"

"Yes."

"Why would someone there want to kill Emile?"

"I don't know."

"According to the news, many people were witnesses, but no one has spoken to the police."

"The no-snitch culture."

"Yes, we have it in Haiti…. I must travel to Port-au-Prince again for a few days. We can talk at length after I return."

Wanting to escape, I stood to shake her hand. She stood, stepped to me and gave me an air kiss, which I wished had been the real thing. I drove home feeling guilty for being sexually aroused by Emile's widow.

8

Next morning, I dressed in faded jeans, a long-sleeved fishing shirt, scruffy boat shoes and my wide-brim fishing hat. In my office, I turned on my phone and studied witnesses, carefully identifying five I would try to interview. I would ask them why they had not spoken to the police and if they planned to. I would be thorough and let each interview take its own course.

I telephoned my cop contact, and he said no witnesses had come forward. After drinking a cup of coffee, I put two sandwiches, a tin of sardines, three Heinekens and two Pepsis in a cooler. Then, I put new batteries for my camera and a roll of toilet paper in my backpack, and I grabbed a plastic milk bottle to piss in. I was prepared to camp out in The Gut Bucket.

I drove my pickup, which I owned to pull the

twenty-foot fishing boat I had recently sold, and parked in the shade of an oak behind the parking lot of the Mall of African Peoples. I had a clear view of almost everyone who entered and exited the businesses through the rear doors. Even at that early hour, old men had gathered under the canopies.

An emergency vehicle flew past, its siren screaming and lights flashing. I turned on my phone gallery and studied photos of my five witnesses. I did not wait long before one, the Well-Dressed Pretty Woman who had screamed and run away when Emile was shot, exited an Audi sedan and entered the beauty salon. I walked to the Audi, photographed the license plate and returned to my truck. After nearly two hours, the woman came out, her hair "done."

She drove away, and I followed her to a ranch house in Shores Golf Resort. She pulled into the driveway, and I parked across the street under a mango tree between two houses. Seconds later, a garage door opened and she drove in. I took a picture of the house and the address. After logging onto the website of the property appraiser, I learned that the address was that of Lela and Javier Snipe. I vaguely recalled his name from a news story.

It was half past noon. I drove around the community for an hour, passing the house several times, hoping that Lela would reappear and I would follow. When she did not reappear, I returned to the Mall of African Peoples, parked in a different spot and ate a sandwich and drank a Pepsi.

It was one of those times when I was glad for the patience I had cultivated over the years as an investigative reporter, when I sometimes waited hours for a two-timing politician to sneak out of his lady's apartment. Working from experience, I was sure I would see my witnesses again, that they would return to their familiar haunt.

9

As I waited, a school bus stopped in front of the convenience store across the street. I looked at the kids disembarking and recognized the Teen Girl who had whispered over Emile's body. She was more delicate-looking than I remembered. Walking in front of the bus safety arm, she wobbled as she carried her oversized book bag and a folded art easel.

Her next move surprised me. She trudged to where Emile had fallen and stared at the spot a long time. I took several photos of her. She turned, adjusted her belongings and trudged toward the apartments two blocks away.

I got out of my truck and followed her to a drab two-story, L-shaped building. I stood behind the fronds of two palms as she took a key from a pocket and let herself into an apartment. She was no older than thirteen, and I assumed she was a latchkey kid. I did not expect a child to go to the police of her own accord, but I hoped that her parents would permit it anonymously. After all, parents with such a lovely child would want a cold-blooded killer removed from their neighborhood.

Moments later, another girl, about eight years old, walked to the same apartment and let herself in. Latchkey sisters. I waited a few minutes, walked close enough to the building to read the numbers on the apartments. They lived in number two. I walked to the mailboxes and saw that number two was rented to Terri Welch.

I returned to my truck and waited. An hour or so later, an attractive brown-skinned woman pulled into the lot and exited a late model Toyota RAV4. She wore a blue lab coat and closed toe white shoes. I could see an I.D. badge on her coat, but I could not read it.

She grabbed a bag of groceries from the back seat,

walked to the apartment and tapped on the door. The girls opened it, jumped up and down and kissed the woman I assumed was their mother. It was a tender moment for me as the door shut behind them.

An hour later, as the sun set, Terri, wearing stylish ripped jeans and a flowered blouse, and the girls left the apartment and walked toward the mall. I drove around the corner and parked as they trotted across the street and entered Just Ribs. I got out and followed.

The place was clean and tidy, its eight tables covered with checkered red, black and green oil cloth. The walls held autographed photos of the many famous entertainers and athletes who ate there. I remembered that it was a required stop for politicians who needed the Black vote.

Two young women took orders at the tables, and an older woman and a young one waited on customers at the counter. I eased onto the last seat at the counter, which had the best view of most diners, and it was

near Terri and her girls, who whispered and giggled.

The older girl said something that made a few people

at nearby tables glare.

"You're too loud, Frida," Terri said to her.

So, you're Frida, I thought. I looked around and

instantly recognized Eugene Tilden, the big man

emerging from the kitchen. He wore the same bib

apron he wore when he ushered Commissioner

Murray inside the day of Emile's murder. He was on

my video, standing in the door, his arms folded over

his chest as he watched Emile die. His face carried

that familiar ghetto Weltschmerz I had learned to

recognize as a child.

I grabbed a menu and half studied it as I listened to

bits of conversations. I looked at Frida, an innocent

child, and I wondered if she could give me insight

into what kids in The Gut Bucket thought about

snitching. What did she whisper over Emile's body?

How many of her acquaintances witnessed the murder, especially her classmates? Did they talk about it? What did they intend to do?

I ordered the brisket plate special and iced tea. Terri and her daughters ordered two slabs of baby back ribs, mac & cheese, collards, corn muffins and lemonade. I ate slowly, eavesdropped and learned that the younger girl's name was Justine. The trio ate ravenously, not so much from hunger as from the pure enjoyment of being together, reminding me that love and innocence did exist in The Gut Bucket. Although my brisket was delicious, I did not finish it because I spent most of the time stealing glances at the trio and trying to no avail to hear more of their conversation.

After getting my food boxed to go, I drove home, showered, poured a large Jack, sat in bed and watched the video over and over. The last thing I remembered before falling asleep was the image of Frida whispering over Emile's body.

10

Early the next morning, I drove to Lela Snipe's house, parked and waited across the street. A few minutes later, the garage door opened, and a late model Range Rover backed out. The man behind the wheel, who I assumed was Javier, drove past without seeming to notice me. The garage door stayed open, and moments later, Lela Snipe appeared wearing business attire. She got in the Audi, backed out, drove past me and waved to a white couple walking a golden retriever.

I followed her to Living in Christ Holiness Church in The Gut Bucket, where she parked in a reserved spot in the staff carport. She walked to the office entrance and let herself in with her key. I parked in the sprawling lot, waited until I thought she had settled into her routine, walked to the office entrance and pressed the buzzer. Moments later, she opened the door wearing a broad smile that I assumed came

with her job.

"Yes, may I help you?" she asked, her eyes lighting

up. "It's Mr. Clary. I recognize you from your picture

in the paper. Please come in."

She led me through the lobby, into her office and

pointed me to a chair beside the desk. The nameplate

read, "Lela J. Snipe. Pastor's Assistant."

"You're our first visitor today," she said. "Sorry

but Dr. Kearse is out of town until Saturday."

"Actually, I came to see you."

Surprised, she walked around the desk, sat and

swiveled the computer screen so that I could not read

it.

"So, Mr. Clary, what's the occasion?"

"I want to talk to you about the murder of Emile

Pomet."

"Oh, God!" she said.

Her hand went to her lips, and she shut her eyes

momentarily.

"I learned that poor man's name on the news," she said.

"Why did you run away?"

She took a deep breath and stood, her hands trembling.

"Coffee should be ready. How do you take yours?"

"Straight up," I said, feeling like a bully.

She hurried away through the lounge door. I got up and walked around the spacious office that had a seating arrangement for meetings and several reading tables with lamps. Shelves held hundreds of books in various disciplines by Black authors, and I realized that the office doubled as a library for parishioners. A brochure indicated that the church, with 4,000 members, had its own publishing imprint.

As I looked around, Lela Snipe returned with two cups of coffee and pastries on a tray and placed the tray on her desk. Having composed herself, she

nodded for me to join her, and we sat facing each
other.

"Mr. Clary, exactly what do you want from me?"

"Why did you run away, and why haven't you gone
to the police?"

"Will this be in the paper?"

"If I write about the murder, your name or any
other personal identifiers won't be mentioned."

She set her cup on the desk and fidgeted.

"When I saw that man killed like that, my body ran
on its own. It was so sudden and violent, I couldn't
think. I went home and stayed in bed until my
husband came. I didn't go to work the next day, the
first time I ever called in sick."

"Why haven't you gone to the police?"

"Javier told me not to."

"Why?"

"Doesn't concern us. He's the compliance officer
for the city department of fleet management. We have

a very good life, Mr. Clary, and we worked hard for it."

"How do you feel about going to the police? Not your husband but you."

"Like I said, our life is good. We have a son who's a senior in high school, and he's been accepted at Yale. Our daughter's graduating from the University of Florida next spring. We won't ruin their lives over this."

"Will you talk to the police anonymously?"

"Nothing's anonymous in Mangrove Shores for Black people in our position. And if I were you, I wouldn't write about that murder. People on the street don't know who you are, Mr. Clary, but others do."

"By 'others' you mean the Black upper crust?"

"Yes, and you're persona non grata."

"I've heard that rumor over the years."

"It's not a rumor."

"Because I write the truth?"

"Your truth."

"Yes, as I know it."

"Truth, per se, isn't the problem. You air our dirty laundry in that newspaper. White people hate us enough as it is. A lot of us object to the same ugly behavior you object to, but we don't broadcast it in a public forum. You shame us, Mr. Clary. That's taboo. Surely, I can't be the first person to tell you this."

"Actually, I hear it all the time."

"And you continue to do it."

"Keeping this stuff in our bedrooms, around the dinner table and on barstools is suicide."

"The Devil will always find work in Cedar Gardens, Mr. Clary. Do you think you help by shaming us? Be honest."

"We can't remain silent about so many bad things before we destroy ourselves. We're committing suicide no matter how you try to rationalize it. We must look at the wheels within the wheels."

She scoffed. "You're full of surprises. Apparently, you've read Ezekiel. But without complete understanding."

"I understand what I've read. We create our own misery by not thoroughly examining our choices, too quick to blame white people, ignoring our self-inflicted wounds at our peril. We must find the courage to be introspective and act accordingly."

We sipped coffee at the same time and set our cups down at the same time, forcing us to smile grudgingly.

"Mr. Clary, it's hard for *real* victims of racism to be introspective the way you're referring to it," she said.

"Not to be flippant but isn't this where prayer can be useful?"

"Exactly where's this going?" she said, her anger growing.

I dropped the introspection angle. "You and your

husband do realize that Emile Pomet's killer is still out there."

"Nothing we can do about that."

"Actually, doing nothing's doing something. It's choosing to let killers go free. You don't feel any guilt about that?"

"I pray on my knees to the Lord about my guilt."

"Do you feel complicit?"

"I pray to the Lord on my knees about my complicity. You were there, too, Mr. Clary. Why haven't you gone to the police?"

"Frankly, I don't know exactly what I'm going to do. But rest assured that as a journalist, I understand my responsibility."

"Which is?"

"To hold wrongdoers accountable," I said, having never uttered those lofty words before. In fact, I did not remember ever thinking such words: *to hold wrongdoers accountable.*

"You see me as a wrongdoer? And do you plan to hold me accountable?"

I was stumped and I was certain my face showed it.

She said, "You don't have to implicate people like me. And if you're looking for absolution, please do it without involving my beautiful family."

Am I seeking absolution? I thought, staring at her Master of Divinity degree from Union Theological Seminary on the wall.

"If we don't start going to the police, Black-on-Black murders become even more depersonalized in The Bucket," I said. "Not going to the police is deliberate indifference. Mass deliberate indifference, in fact. Isn't that a sin in Christianity?"

"You can cherry pick sin if that's your game. And, by the way, this is feeling like a district attorney's interrogation, not a reporter's interview."

Knowing that we were speaking at cross-purposes, I grabbed my phone, walked around the desk, stood beside her, turned on the video and placed it in front of her. She gasped at seeing herself watching the shooting, and she sprang to her feet.

"Oh, God, that's me!" she said, grabbing my hand and continuing to watch herself. "Oh, Jesus!"

I was afraid she was going to faint, so I turned off the video.

"Mr. Clary, please don't destroy my family for what someone else did," she said and let go of me. "I didn't kill that man. I was simply in the wrong place at the wrong time, an innocent bystander."

"There are no innocent bystanders in The Bucket, adult or child," I said, feeling cruel but not enough to back off. "You witnessed a cold-blooded murder.... I know you see yourself as a good person, but you cannot be a good person if you remain silent after witnessing a cold-blooded murder."

"Are you a good person?"

"I used to think so, but I don't know what to think

about myself right now. And, by the way, I don't see myself as an innocent bystander."

Her phone rang, and she looked at the ID and answered.

"Let me call you back," she said, disconnecting and turning back to me, somewhat breathless. "Mr. Clary, please don't destroy my family for what that monster did or just because you have a warped idea of what a good person is. You don't have that right."

Her diploma got my attention again, and it was the perfect time to shift the focus of our conversation before she went into asphyxia.

"Not to pry, but you have a master's in divinity from Union. Why are you just the pastor's assistant and not the assistant pastor? Why don't you have your own pulpit? And how do people address you: Lela, Mrs. Snipe or Reverend Snipe?"

She sighed. "I'll answer your last question first. The women call me Sister Lela. I'm their first responder – spiritually, emotionally, psychologically and otherwise."

"Off the record. What do the men call you?"

"To my face or behind my back?" she said, a crooked smile forming. "It's Reverend Snipe to my face. I won't repeat what some of them call me behind my back. You apparently don't know much about Black Pentecostals. As a woman, I'm invisible in the upper ranks. And no, I don't have a pulpit. I do this job because I love it and because I make a positive difference."

"How should I address you?"

"What feels comfortable?"

"After meeting you, Reverend Snipe feels right."

"You're not all bad," she said chuckling. "You can call me Lela."

"Lela it is. Don't some other Black denominations give women with your credentials real authority?"

"The Methodists do a little better than Pentecostals.

Just a little. The AME and CME disdain us, too. Forget about the Baptists. As bad as it is, Pentecostalism's my calling, my home."

"I understand. I grew up around Holy Rollers."

"Pentecostals. Not Holy Rollers. Obviously, you never spoke in tongue."

"God gave me a defective tongue."

"No, Mr. Clary, your comrade, the devil, did that."

"Whatever," I said, laughing. "I discovered I wasn't Pentecostal material at age twelve."

"Mighty young to learn you're going to hell, isn't it?"

"There was this beautiful girl I had a crush on. She spoke in tongue one Sunday close to midnight, and I ran to the altar and tried to speak in tongue so she would like me. I had foamy saliva pouring from my mouth."

Lela smiled and nodded.

"Don't ask me how I produced all that spit," I said.

"I even conjured up some full-body shaking, twitching and eye-rolling, a masterful performance. Elmer Gantry would've shouted 'hallelujah.' Some of the old folks praised me for being 'saved.' It was all bullshit, of course. After the service, I told the girl how great it felt to be saved, but she called me a 'phony' and laughed in my face. I was so humiliated, I never set foot in another church until many years later, at my parents' funeral."

"Unlike you, Mr. Clary, I spoke in tongue and was saved right after high school."

"Well, my beautiful girl got pregnant in eleventh grade."

Lela's phone rang and she checked the ID. She nodded apologetically, signaling that she needed to take the call. We waved to each other and I let myself out. Seven women waited in the lobby. I said good morning and they returned my greeting.

One said: "Sister Girls, look at that fine specimen

going right there. Praise the Lord!"

They all cracked up and I did, too.

11

At my favorite waterside restaurant, I ate breakfast in a rear booth and studied the remaining four witnesses I wanted to interview. A Young Man on the other side of the crowd, wearing a local university T-shirt, pressed jeans and Gucci sneakers, always caught my attention because of his contemptuous expression. He stayed behind several people, his face lowered as if he was trying to hide. Stealing glances at Emile's body, he seemed totally out of place.

After breakfast, I drove to Aces High Barbershop, hoping that Young Man would show up. It was the barbershop of choice for university Black students. Eleven customers sat in theater-style seats against one wall, and barber chairs were on the other side. I sat in the seat at the end near the bathroom and thumbed through a copy of *Vibe* magazine to keep from sharing direct eye contact with anyone.

The six barbers were busy, and good-natured banter and laughter filled the air. I wondered how many of them had witnessed Emile's killing and were not on my video. I glanced at all of their faces and instantly recognized two. No one seemed to recognize me.

When the owner, Terrell Holmes, entered through the front door, all heads turned and a deferential "Going on, Terrell!" went up. Wearing a coat and tie, he was tall, brown-skinned and handsome. He waved and disappeared into his office. He was on my video watching Emile's killing, his hands on his hips.

The barber in front of me finished a customer and yelled "next." No one else moved so I went to his chair. His name tag read "K Man." After he put the cape around my neck, I asked for a simple trim on the sides, nothing off the top.

"Haven't seen you here before," he said.

"First time."

"Where you from?"

I had learned over the years to stave off risky questions by unloading bullshit upfront, making subsequent questions relate to my bullshit and not to my *real* self.

I said, "Atlanta. I'm what they call a library acquisitions programmer."

"Fuck's that?"

"I sit at a computer and classify journal articles."

"Sounds boring."

"A decent paycheck."

"Still sounds boring."

After he finished my hair, I paid and gave him a nice tip, realizing that interviewing him or anyone else there would be a total waste of time. They would spew the "same old no-snitch crap," in Asa's words.

Not finding Young Man there and still assuming he was a student, I went to the university's main cafeteria for lunch, hoping I would see him or get a lead. I looked around the room before joining the serving line.

About a dozen Black students ate together in a corner behind the salad bar, and a handful of older Blacks like me were scattered about. After paying for my food, I sat at a table where I could clearly see the serving area. A few moments later as I looked around, I saw Young Man outlined against a sunlit window away from where most other Black students sat. He was laughing and chatting with a gorgeous redbone who nibbled edamame. I photographed them with my phone, finished my food, went outside and sat at a table facing the cafeteria's main doors.

Young Man and Redbone came out about thirty minutes later, stopped on the walkway and kissed. Wearing a Balmain denim mini dress, Redbone went into the library, and Young Man walked to the dorm across the street. I stayed close behind him as he entered the lobby. Pretending to read a bulletin board, I could hear him as he spoke to the security attendant, an old white man in uniform behind the counter.

"Anything for me?" Young Man said.

"Be right back, Mr. Oakes," the attendant said.

He smiled and walked through swinging doors behind the desk. He came back with two envelopes and handed them to Mr. Oakes, who dashed to a waiting elevator.

"Can I help you?" the attendant said, turning to me.

I lied, of course. "My daughter will be attending the university next semester, and I want to see where she'll be living."

"A great dorm. Kids from all over the world."

"Looks like that young man loves it," I said, pointing in the direction Mr. Oakes had gone.

"Yeah, Ture. Chicago kid. He loves the weather down here. On the dive team."

I had his name, Ture Oakes, and where he was from. The attendant grabbed a brochure from a shelf and handed it to me.

"We give parent tours by request."

"Excellent," I said. "I'll come back and make an appointment."

I saluted with the brochure and walked out of the building. At the library, I saw Redbone behind the circulation counter. I went into the third floor stacks, grabbed a copy of the book *Crossing the Water and Keeping the Faith: Haitian Religion in Miami* and went to the circulation counter. I could check out books because the university gave local journalists borrowing rights. As I placed my ID and book on the counter, Redbone compared my picture on the card to the man standing in front of her. According to her name tag, she was Yvette Ford.

I wondered if Ture had told her about Emile's killing. At a table, I studied my video to see if I had captured Yvette there. I had not, so I assumed she did not witness the killing. I googled Ture Oakes, and I did not find his name, but I found Antoine and Jean

Oakes of Chicago. Antoine, handsome in his photo, was an economics professor at Roosevelt University, and he had published two books and many journal articles. Ture resembled the man in the photo. Jean, beautiful and laughing, owned a travel agency in Hyde Park, and a photo showed her with a group of Black travelers in Cape Town, South Africa. I found nothing on Yvette Ford.

I looked up from the video just as Yvette disappeared through a door behind the counter. She reemerged moments later carrying her purse and book bag, waved goodbye to her coworkers and walked out of the building. I followed her to the dorm where Ture lived, and because I did not want the dorm attendant to see me again, I stood outside and watched Yvette through the glass wall as she collected her mail and caught the elevator.

It was 4 o'clock, so I decided to have a snack in the cafeteria on the chance the couple would return to eat or hang out with schoolmates. After more than an

hour without seeing them, I assumed they would not

reappear that day and left.

12

At home, I studied the background of another witness I wanted to interview. The next afternoon, I found him, Earl Andrew Gleason, head football coach at predominantly Black Cedar Gardens High School. He was a legend, owning one of the state's winningest records in football. You did not have to say his given name in Mangrove Shores. "Coach" sufficed.

Coach was on my video, standing at the side of Aces High Barbershop blankly watching Dreadlocks shoot Emile. I studied his face and realized that I had never spoken to him and had only seen his photo in the newspaper and heard him on TV and radio.

For three decades, he had sent many football players to colleges and universities nationwide, several of his players having become National Football League standouts. His nickname was "The

Earl of Gleason." I once heard a Black sportswriter say of Coach: "I swear that nigger's got a one-hundred watt halo over his head."

When I phoned him, he vaguely recognized my name and invited me to his office, a cavernous space on the second floor of the gym with a perfect view of the football stadium.

He met me at the door, shook my hand with a bear grip, slapped my shoulder and pulled me to him. I was six feet two inches tall, but I found myself looking up at him.

"Brother Ron Clary," he said, his voice booming. "Come on in. I'm designing some red zone offensive plays. Eat up the clock and score every time."

"That's pretty much the last thirty years."

"We can do better."

"What? Annihilation?"

"Just like Vince Lombardi," he said, grinning. "Well, what can I do for you?"

His demeanor was gruff but not rude as I had expected. In fact, he was a natural-born charmer, forcing me to adjust my attitude. He led me to a recliner, and he sat behind his massive oak desk.

Trophies stood like sentinels in glass cases, and hundreds of players' photos – high school, college, NFL – decorated the walls. Three couches and six recliners for staff meetings were placed in a horseshoe around his desk, and he had a large photo of wife and himself on the desk. It was the only photo of him in the office, a sign that he put his players first, as sportswriters had said over the years.

Conventional wisdom was that he was not "a man to fool with," so I went straight to the point.

"I want to show you something," I said, taking my phone from my pocket and placing it in front of him. I turned on the video, the frames showing him watching Dreadlocks shoot Emile.

He jumped to his feet and pointed at my phone.

"That's me!" he shouted. "Turn it off!"

I did so and he sat, sweating. He stood, not waiting for me to speak, and walked across the room to the window overlooking the practice field. Sunlight outlined his muscled frame and he turned to face me.

"That young man played quarterback for me," he said.

I had a hard time envisioning Dreadlocks as a *young man.*

"The University of Miami offered him a scholarship," Coach said. "He got involved in drugs, and before he could go to Miami, he shot another boy – killed him – and went to prison for four years. Involuntary manslaughter. Never got that scholarship. He was the real deal. NFL material."

"What's his name?"

"Trey Saunders."

Trey Saunders, a real "Christian" name, I thought, having not imagined that this cold-blooded bastard had a real name. Dreadlocks was more than he deserved.

"He still holds the pass-completion record in the county," Coach said. "Damn! He was something. Come here."

I followed him to a glass case where he pointed to a trophy and a photo of Dreadlocks, a smiling kid with an ordinary haircut, his arms raised victoriously for a cheering crowd.

"We went undefeated that year and won the state championship. Trey had it all. He followed instructions and could think outside the box on a thin dime. A natural-born leader. Sometimes, he even went to church with my wife and me and other players. What a waste."

He returned to his chair and sat.

"Do you and your wife still take the boys to church?"

"Why are you really here, to show me that video?"

"That's part of it."

"Okay, I saw it. What else?"

"Trey Saunders killed Emile Pomet in cold blood, and you saw it. Are you going to the police?"

He gave me the look he would give a referee who made a stupid call that cost him a game.

"What the fuck are you talking about?"

"Are you going to turn Trey in?"

He stood and stomped to the window again.

"You expect me to ruin Trey's life?" he said, not hearing the irony in his words. "No way in hell."

"But you saw him kill an innocent man, Coach."

"I didn't know that man."

"That matters?"

He walked back to the desk, stood over me and folded his arms across his chest.

"Brother Clary, Trey was not just one of my players. He was one of my sons. That's how I treat my players, like my own sons. I try to protect them.

You understand that?"

"Do you have biological children?"

"Had a son. Killed in Afghanistan. Marines."

"Sorry."

"You have children?"

"No."

"Married?"

"No."

"Siblings?"

"No," I said, preparing for harsh judgment.

"Your parents living?"

"Both killed in a car wreck."

"Sorry. Who raised you?"

"My fraternal grandparents."

"Got a main lady?"

"No."

"So, there's nobody you really give a shit about."

It was a loaded assessment that made me hesitate

before speaking. I looked at him and detected his

contempt for me beneath that practiced cordiality that had served him so well over the years in securing scholarships for his players and raising money for the school's entire athletic department.

"Actually, I really care about several people," I said, realizing that we were talking at cross purposes.

"Would you do *anything* for them?"

"Do you mean lie or keep silent about a cold-blooded murder they committed?"

"Exactly what I mean," he said, his tone defiant. "A lot of my boys don't know their real fathers, just like Trey. It breaks my heart to say it, but his mom was a coke head and a whore. My wife and I let Trey stay with us whenever his mom went to jail or got evicted. That boy had a hard life. He stayed with us one time for seven months. The judge let us keep him instead of sending him to that juvenile justice cesspool."

"None of that justifies why it's all right for Black people to keep silent when we kill one another. You witnessed a cold-blooded murder, Coach."

"You saw it, too. So you're going to snitch on Trey?"

It was more than a tit-for-tat question. Coach's focus on Trey showed a lack of empathy for Emile and a cynical disregard for simple decency.

"I'm the press, and I'm going to remain objective by listening to witnesses, which includes you, Coach," I said, struggling to control my anger.

"Sounds like bullshit to me. What're you going to do with that video?"

"Not sure. But you need to know there are other copies with instructions in case something happens to me."

"You reporters are slick. Been dealing with you assholes ever since I started doing X's and O's."

For the first time, I noticed his bachelor's degree in math from Florida State on the wall, and he saw my interest.

"Yeah, my real day job's teaching math," he said. "I use math in coaching. Angles and distance, individual players' performance, play-by-play summaries and analyses, opponents' stats. You name it. I use it."

He leaned back and folded his arms. I took advantage of the ease in tension with a question a good cub reporter would ask: "How did a math teacher get involved in coaching football?"

"Hennessy cognac and a barstool," he said, chuckling, which I welcomed. "Thirty years ago, I was at the bar down the street drinking Hennessy and running my mouth with some of the brothers. Our young head coach was there, and he heard me say we lost the homecoming game because he ran the wrong plays on every third down. He'd had a few glasses of Henny, too, and he was pissed and ready to go upside my head.

"He said, 'If you know so much, nigger, why don't

you come out and show me how to run third down plays in the red zone.' Being new on campus, he didn't know I'd been a wide receiver at FSU and knew the game. On my dare, he talked the AD into letting me be an assistant. In no time, he saw I was good with the boys and kept me on. Two years later, he got a new job in Gainesville, and I replaced him."

"Did you work well with Trey, too?"

"I thought I did," he said in a voice of regret.

"I don't mean to be snarky, Coach, but do you teach your boys old-fashioned stuff like good citizenship and personal responsibility, not just running, passing, catching, blocking and tackling?"

"Of course I do. What kind of question is that? For a lot of them, the streets mean more than what I say."

"Do you discuss Black-on-Black crime with them?"

"Not those words. I tell them they shouldn't hurt anybody or gangbang. Always wear a rubber when they screw the sisters. Don't give them a disease and don't get them pregnant."

"What about snitching?"

"What about it?"

"Do you discuss it?"

"I teach them to live good lives," he said, wiping his face with his hand. "You don't understand things around here. White people don't play right. Cops plant evidence and lie and do all kinds of shit to throw us in jail, especially the young brothers like Trey. No, I don't tell them to go to the cops. Why would I do that? We take care of our own problems."

"How? When?"

"What do you mean?"

"Emile was shot down in public. No one has spoken up. A woman was shot dead in her front yard, right up the street. A rapper and three in his group were killed the other night. No one has come forward. That's not taking care of our own problems. If we don't care about ourselves, how can we expect other people to? A Black person here in The Bucket will kill another Black person before the week is out, and the killer won't be reported.

"Our main problem isn't white people. It's us, our silence that amounts to collective self-abasement. Trey should be on death row. He's a pitiless killer. I know white people are bastards, but they always will be. So what are we left with? Ourselves. We have to change ourselves, Coach. We are our own problem. Until we clearly understand that and get some self-awareness, we will remain lost and despised and continue to struggle and suffer. Have you ever thought that we don't belong in this country?"

"I thought we were talking about Mangrove Shores."

"Yes, we're talking about Mangrove Shores, and we're talking about the whole of America and every other place in the universe where Black people live.

We're not wanted."

"Get real. Do you live in the 'hood'?"

"No."

"Well, this is my home. I was born and raised five blocks from here. These are my people. I tore down my parents' old place and built a new house there twenty years ago. When I graduated from FSU, I came home for good."

"You're rare," I said. "Ninety-nine-point-nine percent of Black leaders don't live here, but they give lip service to its virtues. In reality, why would anyone live here?"

"You have a low opinion of us."

"Coach, The Bucket shapes character in mostly bad ways," I said, tired of being labeled an enemy of Black people. "How much do you really know about your players? I mean about what really goes on in their homes. Too many of them wind up gangbanging, behind bars or six feet under before they're twenty."

He remained silent.

I said, "Coach, have you read James Baldwin?"

"Nah, but I saw a movie they made out of one of his books."

"*If Beale Street Could Talk*"?

"Yeah. Students forced me to watch it."

"I mention Baldwin because he was a brilliant observer of Black life."

"Too bad he was a faggot."

"I want to share what he wrote about Black males in his book *The Evidence of Things Not Seen*."

"Why?"

I said the book held meaning for him, explaining that it focused on Wayne Williams, the convicted Black serial killer in Atlanta, in which Baldwin summarizes what Andy Young told him about Black males. Young was Atlanta's Black mayor during the murders that occurred between 1979 and 1981. I

Googled the book on my phone and found the excerpt I wanted.

I read the excerpt: "There is, according to Andy, a disease peculiar to the Black community, called 'sorriness.' It is a disease that attacks Black males. It is transmitted by Mama, whose instinct...is to protect the Black male from the devastation that threatens him the moment he declares himself a man. All of our mothers, and all of our women, live with this small, doom-laden bell in the skull, silent, waiting, or resounding, every hour of every day. Mama lays this burden on Sister, from whom she expects (or indicates she expects) far more than she expects from Brother; but one of the results of this all too comprehensible dynamic is that Brother may never grow up...."

Coach and I stared at each other a long while.

"Damn!" he said, captivated. "Baldwin wrote that? He was saying Black mothers don't let their boys grow up because they're trying to keep them alive. Crazy. But it makes sense. What's the name of that book again?"

"*The Evidence of Things Not Seen*," I said, gathering my belongings and standing. "I'll bring you a copy."

Coach smiled in a way suggesting that he no longer felt under attack and stood.

"One more thing," I said. "If we don't change for the better in significant ways, we'll be lost to history like the Calusa Indians. Gone. Disappeared."

"What?"

"We *must* change, Coach."

"I really don't understand what you're saying, but I do know if Trey gets arrested for killing that man, you'll be the one who snitched."

"More than a hundred other people saw the killing. Could be any one of them."

"No, it'll be you."

"Coach," I said hoping he would pay attention, "because of our silence, we've betrayed generations before us, people like Fannie Lou Hamer and Bob Moses and Stokley Carmichael who risked their lives to get us the simple right to vote. I despise these thugs out there, including Trey. They disgrace our heroes, living and dead. When I came in here, you were devising red zone offensive plays. That's what Black people need, red zone offensive plays."

"What're you talking about?"

"All we do is play defense, reacting to white people. When will we start taking control of our lives, getting on offense and devising ways to take care of ourselves despite white people? White people will be white people, always treating us like shit. Marcus Garvey said: 'Emancipate yourselves from mental slavery, none but ourselves can free our minds.'"

Coach stared at me contemplatively, without a hint of malice. "That makes sense," he said.

"I'll get the James Baldwin book to you tomorrow."

"I feel punched – no kicked – in the gut."

"Sorry, Coach," I said, not meaning it.

We shook hands and I left, trying to feel hopeful.

13

That night, I drove to Just Ribs two hours before closing just as the bail bonds mobile office was exiting the parking lot. I entered the front door, sat at the counter and asked the young woman tidying up if I could speak to the owner. Five other customers ate at the counter without seeming to notice me. The young woman's name tag read "Andrea Cannon."

"May I tell him your name?"

"Ron Clary. I write for the newspaper."

She did a double take.

"Yeah, I recognize you. I'm a student at the university, and we used one of your columns in class, the one about poor service in Cedar Gardens. We had to write about a problem we care about. Hospitality Management is my major."

"So what did you write about?"

She glanced around and whispered: "Shitty

tipping."

We chuckled.

"Are you an intern?" I said.

"No, this is a real part-time job. If I didn't have so many classes, I'd do it full time."

"You like it?"

"Love it. I'm going to open my own place one day, then start a chain."

Her easy demeanor led me straight to the point.

"Were you here when Emile Pomet was murdered the other day?"

"No, my shift doesn't start until five."

"Have you heard people talk about it?"

"No."

"Are you surprised no one's talking about it?"

She glanced around and lowered her voice.

"I'm from Newark, New Jersey, Mr. Clary. It's the same there…. By the way, I know Professor Pomet. My boyfriend took an elective with her. She's a rock star on campus."

At that moment, Eugene Tilden emerged from the kitchen and walked to Andrea. As he was about to speak, she whispered to him, and he looked at me, his expression spiteful.

"Andrea said you want to talk to me. You're from *that* newspaper."

"Can we talk privately?"

He looked at his watch. "A few minutes. Got to go to the wholesale house. Rap concert coming to town."

We went into his cramped office. He sat behind a desk too small for him, and I sat on a metal folding chair. I could smell mesquite wood and the aroma of barbecue seeping through every crack in the place. He noticed my reaction and smiled.

"Best barbecue you ever ate," he said. "But you didn't come to talk about my barbecue."

"True. I want to ask you about the killing the other day."

"What about it?"

"Did you know the victim, Emile Pomet?"

"No."

Because he was abrasive, I wasted no time and took my phone from my pocket, turned on the video and placed it in front of him. He was shocked, and I thought he was going to grab the phone and destroy it. He wiped his brow with the cloth napkin that had been on the desk and stared from the video to me.

I stopped the video and went for the jugular. "Mr. Tilden, do you plan to go to the police and tell them Trey Saunders killed Emile Pomet?"

"Fuck no. I wouldn't snitch on Trey and put myself out of business, you stupid motherfucker." He grabbed my phone and turned it face down. "If you know what's good for you, you'll get rid of that."

"This isn't the only copy."

"Why are you stirring up this shit? Some fucking Haitian bigshot got killed. Had no business dissing

143

Trey in front of his crew."

"Exactly what did the man say?"

"I wasn't there, but everybody said it was fucked up."

"Saying something fucked up is a reason to kill a man in cold blood?"

"Pride, newsman. Pride." He stood and walked to the window and looked out. "Trey will hear about that video."

"So you're not going to the police."

"I don't snitch. You wouldn't understand that. And I'm going to tell you something. A lot of niggers in The Bucket want to get Trey. He makes more money than all these hustlers, and he fucks all the fine bitches. They have to snitch to get him, but they won't do that. When Trey makes money, all these niggers make money. He's the rainmaker in The Bucket. Next week, he's putting on a battle rap concert. Going to bring in rappers from around the state."

He looked at the wall clock again. "Got to get to the meat house. Like I said, Trey will hear about that video."

I stood and handed him my business card. "In case you want to talk again."

He took the card, glanced at it and flicked it onto the desk.

"Come here," he said and walked to the window.

I went to him and he pointed out.

He said, "What do you see?"

It was a sly question, and I knew that any answer I gave would be unsatisfactory.

"Your grill. Your pit. Your pit masters. Your mesquite. That mangy cur in the alley licking his balls."

"That's what I mean about niggers like you. Last time I checked, that was The Gut Bucket out there, but a Negroid like you can't see it. Know why you can't see it? That white newspaper brainwashed your Black ass. You see with white people's eyes, and you think and talk like white people. I see with Black eyes and hear with Black ears. I see my people for *real*. I keep it *real*. We take care of our own shit, and we keep it in The Bucket, in the village."

"The village? Mr. Tilden, if you're talking about this 'it-takes-a-village' crap, you're delusional. It's a handy fiction. If The Gut Bucket's a village, it's a village of the damned, the dysfunctional. Actually, we don't take care of our own shit. A woman, eight months pregnant, was killed in a drive-by two nights ago down the street from here, just standing in her yard talking to a neighbor. Nobody's gone to the police. She had two young children in the house. Those kids are motherless and fatherless."

"Bitch was probably fucking some other lady's old man."

"No, the fool who shot her thought she was the

woman who owed Trey, his boss, money for meth. Wrong woman. Who'll take care of those little kids?"

"Family and friends. You're one of these niggers who won't ever understand."

Since I had him talking, I pressed on at the risk of trading punches or being forced to run and hide.

"Last year, three Black people were shot on Martin Luther King Day during a block party. Do you understand what that means, what it looks like to white people? The cops don't have any leads. We can't let cold-blooded killers walk our streets just because they're Black. White people hate us, but we hate one another more than white people hate us."

He checked his watch, then shook his finger in my face.

"In slavery time, other slaves would've hung your ass from the tallest tree on the plantation because you're a no good nigger."

I waited for him to calm down before speaking.

"I used to be a police reporter. So I know that the majority of people in The Bucket don't commit serious crimes. But a lot of them tolerate and ignore serious crimes and let criminals walk the streets. Just like you, I know we're treated unfairly by agencies and institutions – the police, the courts, banks, housing, car dealers and college admissions. You name it.

"But what does any of that have to do with us blowing one another off the map? Society will never treat us fairly. We're never going to be equal to whites. We need to learn that and live the best lives we can. Too many people here in The Bucket sit around on their filthy asses and don't do shit for themselves. We must treat ourselves better and start caring about ourselves because everything's against us. Mr. Tilden, our problems went out of fashion decades ago. Even *that* God we worship so faithfully hates our asses."

"You one crazy motherfucker."

"Like I said, I was a police reporter, and the scariest thing I learned is that very few cops, white or Black or otherwise, take us seriously. They don't even see us as being human, especially after they handcuff us. We're a joke. They think nothing of killing us, and they laugh at us."

"Laugh at what?"

"All the stupid shit we do to ourselves. I don't know about you, but I don't want white people laughing at us. I'm sick and tired of Black bullshit. It's like a disease. Maybe it is a disease."

He rolled his eyes, and I picked up my phone and notebook from the desk.

"We must stop dehumanizing ourselves if we're ever going to be a viable people," I said.

"Viable? Fuck you talking about? If this is about snitching, I don't want to hear it. Snitching's being a traitor, a fucking Uncle Tom like you."

Although I had always resented being disparaged as being an Uncle Tom, I rarely thought of defending myself by explaining that the real Uncle Tom had been mischaracterized and turned into his opposite.

"Mr. Tilden, may I tell you about the real Uncle Tom?" I said in my best diplomatic voice.

My question surprised him. Like most Blacks I knew, he had not thought of Uncle Tom beyond using it as a vile epithet to attack Blacks like me who were critical of our self-destruction.

"Tell me about Uncle Tom and make it quick," he said derisively.

"He was an actual man, a slave who gained his freedom. He lived from about 1789 to 1883. His name was Josiah Henson, and he was so inspirational that Harriet Beecher Stowe, a white abolitionist, made him the hero of her novel *Uncle Tom's Cabin*. Did you read it in high school here in The Bucket?"

"Nah, our teachers didn't waste time on that crap."

For the next five minutes, with Tilden checking his watch, I told him about Henson, how over many years and at great personal risk, he led slaves to freedom on the Underground Railroad. He was hardly servile and self-loathing in real life, and Stowe did not portray him as such in her novel. That monstrous description of the obsequious nigger was the work of intellectually dishonest white writers who hated Stowe for her anti-slavery crusade. I made it clear that Uncle Tom never personally benefited from snitching on fellow slaves.

"Uncle Tom was a bona fide hero in real life and in the novel," I said. "He never curried the favor of white people for his own benefit. That's contemporary bullshit, and most Black people are stupid enough to suck it up because it absolves them of introspection. In real life and in the novel, Uncle Tom allows himself to be whipped to death rather than reveal the whereabouts of runaway slaves."

"Don't have time for this shit," Tilden said. "Got to get to the wholesale house so I can feed all these rap fans coming to town."

He pointed me from the office. The door slammed behind me, and I stumbled into the semi-lit parking lot where thugs and their retinues milled about. The pit master and his crew were dousing coal and cleaning up. Tilden exited the building, waved to the workers, rushed to the step van and drove away.

Watching him disappear, I decided that I would not let anyone else get away with accusing me of being their version of an Uncle Tom.

During the next few days at home, I transcribed and printed my notes related to Emile, and I read several in-depth articles and a book about snitching. When the reading became too dismal, I took time off to swim, fish and stroll on the shoreline of my apartment. The hot sunrays, cool breezes and salty water were reinvigorating. As birds and boats went

about their routines, I thought again about my
childhood dream of going down to Key West, buying
a fishing boat and living in an airy conch house on the
water.

14

On Monday afternoon, I waited in my car near Frida's bus stop. At 3:40, she stepped off the bus, adjusted her book bag and trudged to where Emile had died. Like before, she stood a long time staring at the spot.

As she walked past my truck, I lowered my head and pretended to be occupied. A few minutes later, I drove to a secluded spot near the apartment and parked. Frida's younger sister arrived and let herself in. As I wrote notes, Terri Welch arrived, parked and went to her mailbox. She retrieved several envelopes but did not look at them. She let herself into the apartment.

I decided to give the family time to complete their after-school and after-work routines. At 6 o'clock, I returned to the apartment, rang the doorbell and waited with conflicting thoughts until Terri asked through the closed door: "Who is it?"

"Ronald Clary, a reporter, Mrs. Welch," I said.

The door opened, the chain in place, and she

peeked out to get a good look at me. I gave her my

business card through the crack. Satisfied, she opened

the door all the way, stepped back and smiled. She

had changed into shorts and a relaxed blouse.

"Mr. Clary, I'm glad to see you," she said, moving

aside.

I walked in and was captivated by the large acrylic

painting on canvas of six Black girls laughing as they

ate mangoes under a tree. It was a colorful work of

joyousness, of the girls exulting in juice smearing

their faces and running down their wrists. I had never

seen an image of such sheer beauty in The Gut

Bucket.

Terri cleared her throat, pulling me out of my

reverie.

"Please have a seat," she said, pointing to the

fabric-covered recliner, the nicest piece of furniture.

I sat in the recliner, Terri on the couch. She looked at me with what I interpreted to be eager expectation. I could hear the girls playing in their bedroom, and I glanced in that direction and again at the painting.

Terri nodded to the painting.

"Frida, my oldest, did it. She named it *Sweet Joy*. She did it in her after-school art class. They showed it at Prentiss Museum, and it won second place. They gave her a certificate."

"I'd love to see what took first place if *Sweet Joy* was second. You said you were glad to see me. Why's that?"

"Aren't you here to talk about the eviction notices? A lot of us called the paper, and they said a reporter was coming. The owner sold our building to a company in Orlando to turn it into retirement condos. We have sixty days to get out. I'm a respiratory therapist with two girls, Mr. Clary, and I can't just pick up and leave. Nobody here can do that."

"I'm sorry, Mrs. Welch, but I'm not here to talk about your building." Seeing her disappointment, I decided to avoid a silly icebreaker and go to the issue. I took my phone from my pocket. "May I sit with you at the coffee table?"

She motioned for me to sit next to her.

"Has Frida talked to you about the murder down the street?"

"You mean that lady shot in her yard?"

"Not that one. The man killed behind Cue Man Pool Parlor."

"She hasn't said anything about that, but I heard about it on TV. Is she in some kind of trouble?"

"No."

"Hard to keep up with the killings around here."

I placed my phone on the table and turned on the video. Terri's fingers went to her lips as the horror of the killing and her child watching it unfolded.

"Oh, my God!" she whispered. "Turn it off." She glanced toward the room where her girls were. "My baby saw that killing. What do you want, Mr. Clary? Why did you show me that?"

"Mrs. Welch, I want to interview your daughter about what she saw and if you will let her speak to the police."

"The police? Are you going to write about her?"

"Not by name if I do. No one will be able to identify her. That I promise and she won't see the video."

"But why would you write about her at all? She's just a child, eighth grade. Don't you have some kind of responsibility to protect innocent children?"

"A man was murdered, and no one has gone to the police."

"People get killed all the time around here."

"That doesn't bother you?"

She stood and walked to the window that faced the

parking lot and stared out.

"My husband, Vic, was killed on 125th Street in Harlem, two blocks from our front door," she said, turning to face me. "He was walking from the subway. He always wore nice clothes, so these punks thought he had money. They killed him for thirty stinking dollars. That's all he had." She caught breath. "His head was in my lap when he said my name and took his last breath. One bullet went through his heart. The other one went through his neck."

"Did they find his killers?"

"No," she said and returned to her seat. "A lot of people saw it, but nobody talked to the police. That's Harlem. I was six months pregnant with my youngest. After I buried Vic, I started a support group for Harlem ladies who lost loved ones on the streets. We met in my living room. Before Vic was killed, I didn't pay attention to the killings because we weren't involved. At first, seeing all those other women was kind of comforting, but the bodies kept piling up on the street. I got madder and madder, and I told the women to stop coming because it was a waste of time.

"No witnesses snitched, and I was hurting. I didn't want to live without Vic, and I thought about suicide, then revenge. A neighbor took me to church one Sunday, and for a short time, I thought I felt better. It didn't work. I got madder at God each time I remembered Vic's blood coming out of his neck and heart. Why did God let that happen? I never went to church again, and I never will. I had a classmate at City College in nursing school who had moved down here. She said the weather was great year-round and the apartments were affordable. She helped me get a job at the hospital where she worked, so I moved."

"You don't care about these killings?"

"We don't get involved in all this Gut Bucket stuff,

Mr. Clary."

"Well, may I talk to Frida?"

"I wish you wouldn't, but it's up to her."

She went to the girls' bedroom, and when she and
Frida emerged, Frida wore baggy shorts and an Andy
Warhol T-shirt. She reluctantly followed her mother
to me. I stood and extended my hand to her, which
she accepted demurely.

I remembered that I had not mentioned the parental
consent form as Terri returned to the couch. As Frida
grabbed a straight-back chair and sat in front of me, I
took the consent form and a pen from my briefcase
and handed them to Terri. She reluctantly signed the
form. I put it in my briefcase and looked into Frida's
sweet face.

She smiled and said: "You're the man in the
newspaper."

"You know who I am?"

"We read your article about kayaking in Osprey

Bayou."

"Have you gone kayaking there?"

"Yes, sir. We did a field trip after we read your article."

"Did you enjoy the field trip?"

She became animated. "We paddled all around the bayou, and we saw three manatees. They were so big and scary-looking. Our teacher said they won't hurt people, but people kill them with motorboats and pollution."

Her field trip experience made me reluctant to discuss the horror of Emile's killing.

"I'm glad you read my column," I said. "But I want to talk to you about the man you saw get killed the other day. Will you tell me about it?"

She looked at her mother, then back to me.

"I saw Trey shoot that man," she said, her lips trembling.

"Do you know Trey?"

"No, sir, but I see him sometimes. People are scared of him – grown people."

Terri touched Frida's hand to comfort her, then said: "Nobody messes with Trey if they know what's good for them."

I acknowledged Terri's comment with a nod, then turned back to Frida. "Will you talk to the police anonymously?"

She stared at her mother, her expression indicating that she was unsure of what "anonymously" meant.

"It means unknown, honey," Terri said. "The police won't know your name. Mr. Clary, I won't let her talk to the police because they can't guarantee anonymity. That monster would kill my baby if he found out."

"I understand," I said and shifted the focus. "Frida, what did you say when you were standing over the man?"

Terri let go of her daughter's hand.

"I told him people shot my daddy in Harlem. I told

him I was sorry that Trey killed him, and I said his family would miss him. That's all. He didn't do anything to Trey. And that boy took that man's watch. Why did he do that?"

She sobbed again, hugged her mother, said goodbye to me and returned to the bedroom. I gathered my belongings.

"I'm sorry, Mrs. Welch," I said, standing. "I will not put Frida's name in the paper, and I hope you all find a nice apartment. Call or email me if you ever want to."

"I'm glad you came by. I don't think Frida ever would've told me about what she saw, and I never would've known what was bothering her. Funny how life works out. I left Harlem to get my girls away from the thugs and murderers. The Gut Bucket is just like Harlem, just smaller. I feel so bad that I brought my babies here."

"I hate to tell you, but the 'hood is the 'hood

everywhere."

"I know that now."

"Tell Frida she's going to be a great artist."

"I will. And thank you."

I placed my business card on the coffee table, said goodbye and left.

15

I was eating breakfast the next morning at the university's main cafeteria and skimming the newspaper when Yvette and Ture sauntered in a few moments apart, met in the serving line and got breakfast. They found a secluded table and sat side-by-side, too far away for me to eavesdrop. They ate quickly, kissed and parted, then off to classes.

I followed Ture to the marine science complex and entered the main door behind him. He chatted with a fellow student near a display of sonar equipment. Moments later, dozens of other students and staff appeared in the corridor and filed into the main lecture hall. I approached the security guard and showed him my press ID. He recognized me and let me enter without my having to lie.

Although there were more than two hundred people there, I spotted Ture immediately in a middle row. He was one among a handful of Blacks, and I found a seat directly behind him.

The professor wasted no time beginning the lecture on red tide, and Ture took meticulous notes. When the lecture ended, I followed Ture to a classroom. The sign on the door read: "Biological Oceanography." I did not try to enter because I would be noticed. For the next ninety minutes, I skimmed books and magazines in the lobby. When the classroom door opened, students filed into the corridor, and Ture headed for the exit. I followed and called to him before he reached the street.

"Hello there," I said. "May I ask you a few questions about your class?"

He turned and faced me. "How's it going?" he said, adjusting his books.

"Exactly what's biological oceanography? I saw the sign on the classroom door."

He wore a university sweatshirt, chino khakis and

expensive top-siders. "You want the catalogue version or the taproom version?"

"Taproom."

"It studies the histories and dynamics of marine organisms over time and space," he said, seeming to enjoy himself.

"If that's the taproom version, I'd hate to hear the one in the catalogue."

He laughed.

"Oh, I'm Ron Clary," I said. "I write for the local newspaper."

His expression growing wary, he shifted his books to the other hand.

"How did you get interested in biological oceanography?" I asked, determined to hold his attention as we walked.

"I grew up in Chicago and spent a lot of time on Lake Michigan with my family on our boat. I love marine life. My high school counselor said Florida's a great place to study."

"Lake Michigan isn't exactly the Atlantic Ocean or the Gulf of Mexico."

He chuckled. "No, but it's the fifth largest lake in the world by surface area."

"I didn't know that."

"Great fishing, too. Anyway, I'm going to get a doctorate and do oceanographic policy and work for EPA."

Listening to him, I was reluctant to bring up Emile's killing because I hated being the cynical intruder who disrupted, at least temporarily, the young man's charmed life.

"Actually, I want to talk to you about a matter unrelated to oceanography," I said. "You're part of a story I'm looking into. Let me buy you lunch."

"You don't even know me. How can I be part of some story of yours?"

"Trust me. You're part of it."

He checked his watch. "Can't we talk right here?"

"This is really sensitive, and it won't take more than a burger, fries and a couple of beers apiece. On me."

"All right. I don't have another class, just diving practice. Let's go to the Snook Hook."

"By the way, what's your name?" I asked, hoping he would think our meeting was chance.

"Ture Oakes."

"Well, to the Snook Hook, Ture Oakes."

The place was packed inside with the early lunch crowd, so we went outside and sat under an umbrella on the patio facing the city harbor. A student waiter followed us and we placed our orders. After a few minutes, the extreme heat explained why the outside tables were mostly empty.

"I've only talked to one reporter in my life, a white chick from the *Chicago Tribune*," he said. "She stopped me in the Loop and asked me if I supported

Black Lives Matter. Of course, I told her. She went stupid and asked me if I thought Black lives matter more than white lives. I asked her if she thought white bitches' lives matter more than Chinese bitches' lives. She told me to fuck off. I told her I'd rather fuck her because she was cute and looked like she could use a good Black fuck."

"I want to ask you about the murder you witnessed a few days ago behind Cue Man Pool Parlor."

His jaws tightened. "You following me?"

"Sort of."

"Another stupid reporter," he said and stood.

"Wait. I need to show you something."

"What the fuck can you show me?"

I motioned to his chair. "Please sit."

He sat grudgingly and glared. I turned on the video and placed the phone in front of him. His impatience turned to consternation as he saw himself standing a few yards from Dreadlocks firing the weapon.

"Shit," he muttered and looked around for observers. "I forgot about that."

I turned off the video and placed the phone face-down on the table.

"You forgot a man was murdered in front of you?"

"I have classes and diving to worry about, not that kind of stuff."

"I thought Black lives matter to you," I said, knowing it was a mocking statement.

"What're you talking about?"

"You saw a Black man shot down by another Black man, but you don't even think about it."

"Hey, I didn't shoot him. I didn't commit a crime, so why're you bothering me?"

"You witnessed it," I said, regretting the hostility I had unleashed.

"No cops have asked me anything," he said.

"Would you talk if they did?"

He looked at my phone. "Are you going to show

them that video?"

Our orders arrived, and I knew he was not going to walk away at that point because seeing himself on the video had unnerved and trapped him. He looked at his food and sipped his beer. For the first few moments, we ate in silence. My grouper sandwich, slaw and hush puppies were delicious, and Ture's nervousness showed as he nibbled his burger and fries.

"What are you going to do with that video?" he said.

"All depends."

"On what?"

"One person snitching."

"Why don't you snitch? If I'm guilty of something, you're guilty of the same thing, even more. You have that video, and it gives you power over other people's lives. You can ruin people with it. What kind of weird shit are you up to? Pulitzer Prize or something?"

For one of the rare times in my life as a journalist, I

did not have an answer about my own behavior that I would print. On the simplest level, my claim to have been following the journalism rule of not being part of the story you write, which I took seriously, was not passing the smell test to my liking.

So, what *really* kept me from snitching? The young man had seriously challenged me, but I would not acknowledge it to him.

"Not to sound corny, Ture, but I must maintain journalistic objectivity in how I treat material," I said, watching his facial expression.

"Always?"

"I certainly try."

"Reporters lie about Black people and withhold information and ruin their lives just like cops do."

"I haven't ruined anyone's life."

He watched me curiously as I hailed our waiter to bring two more beers.

"Have you discussed the murder with anyone else –

friends, your lady, your parents or schoolmates?" I asked.

"Fuck no. Why would I?"

My face must have shown distress over his reply because he raised a brow and sat back. The waiter brought our beer and the check, and I handed him my credit card.

"What good would it do if I snitch?" Ture said. "I'm from Chicago. There are killings in Bronzeville, West Garfield Park, Washington Park, Englewood, and, I mean, you name the 'hood. Niggers don't give a shit about one another in my hometown, so why should I give a shit about this place? What if I did care? Would it matter? What're you upset about? These people will go on killing. Somebody will get killed this weekend in The Bucket. It'll happen in Chicago, Atlanta, Miami, Detroit, Harlem, Syracuse, Oakland, Houston and New Orleans. Everywhere.

"I'm not going to screw up my life by going to the

police, answering a bunch of hostile questions, picking niggers out of a lineup, going to court, getting my face on TV and in the newspapers and having to hide under my bed because I snitched. Who's going to come to my dorm to help me when these thugs come to kill me? Will you rescue me, Mr. Ron Clary? I don't want to get blown away over shit that's not my business. I don't know any of these people, and I don't want to know them. The only thing I have in common with them are race and residence on planet Earth." He glared at me. "Mr. Clary, these niggers don't give a fuck about anything of value. Do you give a fuck or are you just getting paid to do a write-up about that dead Haitian?"

"I actually give a fuck, Ture," I said, again feeling my motives being challenged by someone half my age, who lacked my life experiences.

The waiter returned, I signed the check and nodded thanks. Ture stared at me, probably bracing for more of my bromides, I thought. He placed his elbows on the table and leaned toward me.

"You didn't kill that man. You didn't pay anybody to kill him. You're innocent, like me. Why do you give a shit, and what're you trying to prove anyway?"

"I'm not trying to prove anything, merely searching for answers. As far as innocence goes, I'm not innocent, and neither are you. No silent witness is innocent. Maybe you can answer this one: Why do Black people, including you, blithely tolerate Black-on-Black murder?"

"Blithely?"

"Casually accept."

He stared into my eyes and placed an elbow on the table.

"Like my father said, we just don't care about one another. We go to church and pray and all that, but it doesn't matter one second after benediction. We're petty and mean, and we treat one another like shit."

I agreed with everything he said, but I played the objective journalist. "You really believe all that?"

"Fucking A," he said and gulped beer.

"What does your mother think of the plight of Black people?"

"Why're asking about my mother?"

"Because you mentioned what your father thinks, I want to know what your mother thinks," I said. "By the way, our women are the only *real* hope for us, the Black race."

"My mom works hard and takes great care of us. She was born in Kenwood, not far from President Obama's old house. She doesn't have time for bullshit. She says ignorance and stupidity and victimhood are a pandemic in the 'hood. If you're sane, you just get out."

"If you could talk to the police anonymously, would you snitch?"

"Wouldn't take the chance. I don't trust the police.

And I wish you wouldn't *out* me with that video."

Since he did not make a move to leave, I risked another question. "If you dislike The Gut Bucket so much, why do you go there?"

"Best haircut in town. I hate it over there just like I hate the ghettos in Chicago. No place to live. Filth and trash and junk everywhere. Illegal businesses. Hustlers. Drugs. Gangbangers. Whores. Ignorance. Crazy people walking the streets. After I go there, it takes me two or three days to decompress.

"My father says most ghetto Blacks want to live the way they live because it gives them freedom. No responsibilities. There's comfort in being officially neglected and forgotten. Keeps you invisible. He calls it 'perverse freedom.' Snitching means giving up that freedom. It brings in the cops, the courts, social workers and do-gooders, researchers, charities and self-righteous reporters like you. Most ghetto Blacks don't want all that normal shit. They want to be left the fuck alone. Free. That's hard for most other people to believe."

"What do you think about Black politicians who represent the ghettos?"

"What about them? They just want to get re-elected. Show me any real improvements Black politicians have brought to The Gut Bucket or any other ghetto?"

"I can see you've thought a lot about this. How old are you?"

"Twenty."

"I'm impressed."

"Whatever. Tell you something else. This street-life pride these thugs brag about is rat poison. It rots their insides and turns them into sociopaths. They hurt a lot of innocent Black people. Nothing about thug life has value. White people go slumming just to see niggers acting out. Guess what we do? Act out for them. When are we going to learn? Martin Luther King and all those civil right activists didn't go to jail, get

chewed up by German shepherds, get knocked down

by fire hoses and get killed for all of this stupid shit."

We sat in silence looking into each other's eyes for

an embarrassingly long time. Our talk was finished

and we knew it. We also knew that we would never

speak at length again, except by chance. We stood at

the same time, shook hands and headed for the door,

shoulder-to-shoulder, without another word.

Sick to the stomach, I trudged down to water's

edge to be alone. As I watched gangly brown pelicans

dive for food, Ture's question rang in my ears: *Why

don't you snitch?*

Had my many years of observing the underbelly of

Black life made me too cynical to care? The longer I

walked and thought, the more clearly I understood

what I wanted: Instead of police forensics identifying

Emile's killer, I wanted Gut Bucket residents to bring

Dreadlocks to justice. I wanted a witness to snitch,

either anonymously or on the record, because that was the only way to address what Ture's father referred to as "perverse freedom."

If no one snitched and Dreadlocks walked free, how should Gut Bucket residents be judged? Yes, I was a witness. But, I told myself, I was a self-aware witness. My silence was not out of fear or apathy or indifference. It was a process of wait-and-see, an essential part of being an objective opinion columnist.

Still, I was feeling like a caricature of Diogenes of Sinope, futilely searching for one honest man.

16

Driving away from the University, I looked in my rearview mirror and saw Dreadlocks' lowrider several vehicles behind. The son of a bitch had been tailing me, and I did not know how long. Eugene Tilden apparently had told him about me and the video. I could not make out his passenger, but I assumed it was Giant Thug. I wanted to go to my apartment for some respite, but I also wanted to prevent Dreadlocks from knowing where I lived.

At the first traffic light, I went through on the caution signal, and the red light and other vehicles stopped Dreadlocks. Moments later, I turned into the alley behind condos under construction, stopped between two huge dumpsters and waited.

When he did not appear after about fifteen minutes, I drove from the alley and headed for a tavern in the arts district that was popular with journalists. I knew it would be busy, which is what I wanted with Dreadlocks tailing me. He would not confront me in an upscale place serving mostly white customers. So Ironic: The presence of white people would protect me from my fellow Blacks.

The building was airy and had a large patio under sprawling oaks. I backed into a parking spot in case I had to make a fast getaway. This was not the first time I had been followed by a disgruntled subject but never by a cold-blooded murderer who would kill me because I could send him to death row.

I sat at a corner table so that I could see my car and others that came and went. I was not hungry but I wanted a drink. When I saw Taylor, an older Black man who had waited tables there for many years, I raised my hand. He recognized me and immediately came over.

"Going on, Ron?" he said. "Touch of Jack?"

"Two touches."

"Niggas dropping like flies over in The Bucket. Been trying to find another place to live. Gunshots almost every night. Niggas gone crazy, but my old lady won't move. She was born and raised over there. Eats, sleeps and breathes that church."

"Reverend Murray's church?"

"Yeah," he said, looking around and realizing that he was spending too much time with me. "Better get them two touches."

He hurried away, and I surveyed the patio and was surprised to see Doris Myers and her videographer at a nearby table eating lunch. I considered trying to sneak out but was afraid they would see me, and I would look like the "asshole" some TV folks had accused me of being.

As Taylor approached with my bourbon, Doris looked around and saw me, her face lighting up. The videographer also saw me and gave me stink eye. I paid Taylor and he left. Doris jumped to her feet and

slunk to my table, her hip touching my elbow. I
inhaled her Yves Saint Laurent Black Opium
perfume, looked into her pleasantly tanned face and
realized anew that she was a sexy flirt.

She said, "Come join us, handsome. And don't tell
me you're waiting for someone or about to leave."

"Actually, I was waiting for someone and about to
leave."

She glanced at my untouched drink. "I'll let you off
the hook this time if you'll answer two questions."

"Since I can't perjure myself, ask away."

"Do you like me?"

"In a manner of speaking."

"Do you find me attractive?"

"Sure," I said, thinking she really would be superb
in bed.

She hip-bumped my arm.

"I've got to tell you, Ron, you're wasting your
good looks at that bird cage liner they call a

186

newspaper. You should be in front of a camera anchoring your own show. Have you ever thought about TV?"

"Low-grade ego."

"Such a waste."

I glanced at the videographer who was giving me intense stink eye. Doris noticed and smiled.

"Her name's Bari Hall," Doris said. "A real sweetheart."

"Yeah, sure," I said, downed my Jack and stood. "Looks like my subject isn't coming."

"Are you writing about the Pomet murder?"

"Probably."

With that, I said goodbye and walked to my car, all the while looking for signs of Dreadlocks. Seeing nothing suspicious, I drove around town for nearly two hours, checking my mirrors. I stopped often, waited and watched.

To be safe, I stayed away from my apartment, and I

booked a room for two nights at the beachside Hilton

because I knew that Dreadlocks and his thugs lacked

the patience to wait me out or attack me there.

17

After I settled into bed and flicked on the TV, Alphonsine telephoned. Along with being surprised, I felt my chest and shoulders tighten with anxiety the moment I heard her voice.

"So, Ronald, how have you been in my absence?"

"Fine," I said, sitting up against two pillows. "Are you back in the States?"

"Just arrived in Miami."

"I expected you to be gone much longer."

"I managed the most difficult tasks before leaving the U.S. – cremation, purchasing an urn and hiring a boat for the cremains. Getting these matters done in Port-au-Prince would've been a nightmare, especially cremation."

"That's right. The body must stay whole for the spirit to transfer into the afterlife."

"Alas, Ronald, voodoo and spirituality permeate

every part of Haitian existence. Emile and I agreed on our final rites years ago, and my relatives promise to respect my wishes. Of course, I won't be around to insist."

"I'm glad you returned safely."

"Which is why I telephoned," she said, an airport loudspeaker blasting in the background. "There are only three weeks left in the semester, and I'll be returning to Port-au-Prince shortly afterward. I would like to do our formal interview as soon as convenient for you."

"Why don't I call you tomorrow and we can set a time and place," I said, remembering that she was still in mourning.

"My home as before?"

"Yes. You really are returning to Haiti permanently."

I heard anguish as she sighed.

"I have no reason to stay in the U.S. I can do more

for the arts in the homeland by being there. Emile and I had always planned to return. He would build beautiful buildings, and I would paint and teach and adopt talented girls."

"Did you ever plan to have your own children?"

"Ronald, Emile and I wouldn't condemn children to life in Haiti, the same as we wouldn't condemn them to life in America."

"What would keep you here?"

"Can you bring back Emile?"

"Please forgive my stupid question."

"There's nothing to forgive. As I said, Emile and I had planned to return to Port-au-Prince. I won't betray him."

"Can you *really* betray the dead?" I said, realizing that I was being harsh. "Would Emile want you to return to Haiti without him, back to so much suffering?"

She paused a long while. "Have you been to the

place where Emile was killed?"

"I've been there."

"The owner asked him to renovate his 'little billiards concern,' as Emile referred to it. He was determined to make it a showcase. Are you a billiards player?"

"No. But I love the physics and art in the game."

"Emile was an excellent player. Sometimes he – what do you all call it? – ran the table. I can't imagine why someone would kill him…. I have to go now. Uber awaits."

"I'll see you in a few days."

"I'm looking forward to it."

We said our goodbyes.

For two days, I read, sipped bourbon, half-watched 1950s noirs on Turner Classic Movies, sat on the balcony and enjoyed the Atlantic surf. All the while, I thought of my next move with Dreadlocks.

As I checked out of the hotel, I looked around the

lobby for signs of threat. I could have used electronic checkout in my room, but I wanted to see if anyone waited for me. Because almost everyone was white and because no one seemed to notice me, I felt relatively safe and caught the elevator to the fourth level to my car.

Out of caution, I drove around for an hour, and I did not detect any tails. At my apartment, I parked in the alley, walked to the side of the building and looked up and down the street. Seeing nothing out of the ordinary, I entered my apartment through the garage door, sat at the living room window for half an hour and observed traffic. Most of it was familiar, neighborhood residents and out-of-towners relishing the scenic view and imagining living in paradise.

My sense of security faded when Dreadlocks' lowrider cruised past, its engine growling. When I saw Dreadlocks and Giant Thug staring at my building, I eased away from the window. I went into my office, sat at my desk, opened the bottom drawer and retrieved my Smith & Wesson M&P. I had not looked at it for more than a year, nor had I seen the two hundred rounds of polymer insert hollow point in the field ammo box in my bedroom closet.

I spent an hour cleaning and polishing the weapon, and I vowed never to leave the apartment without it being either in my briefcase or glove compartment or on my person as long as Dreadlocks was a threat. My concealed carry permit was good for another three years.

Although I disliked firearms, having to conduct my own investigations for my columns, sometimes in dangerous circumstances, taught me to be prepared for people who would shoot me or have me shot to keep their names and mugs out of the news.

My simple life was gone. I had created the prospect of a life-or-death showdown with a cold-blooded killer and decided to renew my shooting skills. I changed clothes and drove to the shooting range where I had qualified for my permit. After four hours there, I left feeling competent again.

As for Dreadlocks, I knew it was not a matter of *if* he would confront me but *when* and *where* and with how much firepower.

Back at home, I loaded the gun and secured it in my ankle holster, my preferred way to carry. I drove to the Mall of African Peoples, and the parking lot had its usual thugs and old men. I parked near the first gazebo, and Deadlocks' car was in its spot between Cue Man and Just Ribs.

Sitting in my truck and surveying the crowd, I spotted several witnesses to Emile's killing. Although I did not think anyone recognized me, I reminded myself that Black ghetto dwellers learn in early childhood to transform like chameleons, changing expressions and poses, making it virtually impossible for outsiders to know what was happening. It was all about self-preservation and leveraging opportunities.

As I was about to exit my truck, my phone rang. It was Alphonsine, and I was surprised to hear reggae thumping in the background.

I said, "Hello, professor. Do I hear Wyclef Jean?"

"Yes. Emile knew Wyclef and loved his music. Now, it means a lot to me."

"I'll make sure that's in my column: the builder and the rapper."

"Yes, but make it the builder and the rap artist."

"Artist, of course," I said. "I want to do the interview in your office at the museum. The setting alone expresses the essence of your life and work."

I also knew that Dreadlocks would not come to the museum.

"Excellent," she said. "Half past noon tomorrow. We can dine while we talk."

We said goodbye, and I turned back to the immediate problem of facing Dreadlocks on neutral territory, away from my home and especially away

from Alphonsine's home.

18

I waited in my truck a few more minutes in case Dreadlocks walked out of Cue Man. When he did not come out, I entered the building. Wearing an Armani slim-fit silk shirt and casual dress pants, he stood at a table preparing to break when he saw me and lowered his cue stick.

He said, "Motherfucker, what you doing bringing your ass in here?"

"You drove past my house this morning, so I figured you wanted to see me," I said, watching Hoodie and Rasta inch closer.

The room fell silent.

Dreadlocks placed his cue stick on the table and walked close enough for me to smell that skunky odor of pot on his clothes and breath. I assumed that he, like most of his thugs, could not start the day without a few tokes. I stepped back, nearly bumping into

Giant Thug who had just slouched in.

"Outside," Dreadlocks said, nodding to make a performance of his authority.

We went outside and stood next to his lowrider. Glancing back, I saw Giant Thug at the window watching us.

"Gene told me about that video. I want it. I'll tell you when and where to meet me."

He smirked in that cocky thug way and glared. I knew the tactic well, meant to put him in control. What he did not know was that as a born-and-bred ghetto nigger, I was unafraid of his kind.

"Nigger, what're you trying to prove?" he said. "That funny-talking Haitian motherfucker kin to you or something?"

"No, and he didn't deserve to die like that."

"That fool dissed me. Strutting 'round with his legal pad and calculator and measuring tape and shit. Ignoring me and my bros. I asked him what he was doing. Nigger said, 'Sir, you need to consult the owner. I'm not at liberty to discuss his business affairs.' That fucking accent pissed me off, too. Turned his back on me. You don't do that shit."

"You killed a man for those silly reasons?"

"Pride, nigger. What the fuck you think? My bloods laughing and shit. Disrespect. You don't dis a nigger in his own house. That goes for you, too, newspaper motherfucker."

I could not count the times I had seen and heard such nonsense as a reason to maim and kill. Nothing substantive was at stake, just pumped-up reputation, bloated self-image and a warped definition of manhood. Real and perceived insults and slights had to be rectified, preferably with violence.

"Was the owner there?" I asked, wondering why he had not intervened.

"Fuck if I know. You going to snitch on me, nigger?"

"I was hoping somebody else would."

"Who?" he said, his tone indicating that he could not imagine anyone snitching on him. "You know what snitches get?"

I nodded.

He said, "Wasting my time with your newspaper ass."

He was angry and feeling vulnerable, and I was worried that he might grab his gun before I was ready to defend myself. I was certain the bulge under his shirt on his right hip was the handgun he shot Emile with. Thugs like him rarely went unarmed. He involuntarily touched the bulge, his fingers massaging whatever was there.

Having surveilled his home several times and taken photos, I decided to give him a personal scare by attacking his sense of invincibility.

"I know where to find you," I said. "Last house on the right on Blossom Lane. A loquat and two foxtail palms in the front yard, and there's a broken sprinkler head. You ought to fix it if your beautiful lady wants to keep those begonias looking nice. Oh, and stop leaving that pit bull's shit in the yard. Pick up behind his filthy ass."

He was shocked. "You been near my house, motherfucker?"

"I'm a reporter, remember?"

"Stay away from my place or you're dead," he said, glancing in the direction of his house, probably wondering how close I had been to his Nubian Queen and his daughter.

I had graduated from being a mere nigger who sold my soul to a white newspaper to being a mortal threat. I felt the weight of the pistol on my leg as he moved his hand off the bulge under his shirt and folded his arms over his chest. Just then, Giant Thug hurried to us. He pulled Dreadlocks aside and whispered something.

"What the fuck?" Dreadlocks said. "Got your piece?"

"Right here," Giant Thug said, touching the gun under his shirt.

"Let's go!" Dreadlocks said.

Forgetting about me, they ran to the lowrider, got in and roared out of the lot. Whose life is about to end? I thought.

19

Sipping bourbon at my desk that night, I tried to process my crisis with Dreadlocks. Just kill him, I thought. Walk up behind him and blow his fucking head off. Then cut off his dreads and deliver them in a garbage bag to his Nubian Queen and daughter.

I removed the pistol and holster from my leg and placed them on the desk. There I was, an ordinary newspaper columnist with an ugly killing device staring at me. The irony was that I was meeting Alphonsine the next day to formally interview her for my column about her husband's extraordinary life.

As I stared at the gun, everything seemed futile, so I took an oil wipe from the cleaning kit and groomed the pistol, realizing that I was trying to quell my increasing anxiety. I re-holstered the weapon and placed it in the bottom drawer out of sight.

I turned on the video of the murder and studied

faces, guessing ages, deciphering reactions, determining how far away people were from the shooting, and, most painfully, examining the faces of the children. Unlike the adults, they peered around, seeming to be aware that they were observing *something* evil.

My hope, which came to me unaccountably, was that they would become better adults than those in The Gut Bucket. One boy, very dark and skinny, gazed at a bearded old man as if seeking the proper way to respond to what was unfolding. The old man did not return his gaze.

Disgusted, I flicked on my favorite local news channel and was stunned to see footage of earthquake devastation in Haiti. I had been so focused on Emile's killing, I had ignored everything else in the news. I watched in disbelief as poorly clad Haitians used their hands and shovels and pickaxes to remove bodies from beneath debris and earth.

A reporter described "the far-reaching impact of the 7.2-magnitude quake that will change the face of southeastern Haiti forever. Many towns have disappeared, and authorities expect the death toll, now at two thousand, to rise as recovery teams venture past violent gangs into the mountains."

I telephoned Alphonsine and she answered on the third ring.

"Hello, Ronald, I was about to dial you," she said, her TV playing in the background. "I want to make sure you come tomorrow. I was afraid you would think I would postpone our interview because of the misfortune in my homeland."

"You read my mind."

"I'm looking forward to our talk. I've gathered some materials."

We said goodnight, and I returned to watching images of hell in Haiti.

I drove to the museum the next day, all the while

checking my mirrors. I did not want to bring Gut Bucket thugs to the museum. After parking, I studied vehicles and everyone nearby before walking to the building.

Alphonsine's office was spacious and well-lit and suitably appointed for her, the professor, the researcher, the public lecturer and the "arts personality" as some journalists referred to her. Lunch was ready when I walked in: marinated pan-fried chicken and walnuts on a bed of onions, peppers and tomatoes. After we dined, Marie Louise, beautiful and dark-skinned, and her two young assistants cleared the table and quietly left, leaving Alphonsine and me alone in the sunlit room.

"Come," Alphonsine said, leading me to a glass table. "How was your meal?"

"Delicious."

"Marie Louise's restaurant, all Haitian cuisine, will open in two weeks. It will be downtown."

"Not in Cedar Gardens?"

"Not in Cedar Gardens," she said, frowning and motioning for me to sit.

I sat, placed my voice recorder on the table and turned it on.

"Some things have changed since we last spoke," she said.

"The earthquake?"

"Yes. I won't be returning to Haiti as soon as I'd planned. Emile's company has been operating a disaster relief program here since the last major earthquake, and I need to find a new director to continue that work. We have a warehouse, which, I'm ashamed to say, I visited for the first time last night. It was Emile's work and I stayed out of it. There are stockpiles of food, over-the-counter medicines and other medical supplies, children's books, clothes, bedding, tents, batteries, generators, flashlights, soap, bottled water, feminine hygiene products, baby food, just about everything. We use charter airplanes and boats to move the supplies. When we're finished here, I'll show you the warehouse and perhaps one of the planes departing."

"I'm impressed just listening to you."

"What I'm about to tell you isn't for your commentary," she said. "I've learned that Emile's timepieces are worth about four million dollars. I'll use the funds to create a foundation to continue his relief work. He left instructions in his will, which I didn't read until now because I never thought he would die. So silly of me."

"Would it be much of an exaggeration if I referred to Emile as a saint?"

"Emile was not a saint, not the Christian kind," she said. "He was an atheist who did great work out of a sense of duty to fellow humans. He believed that our tiny homeland of eleven million is cursed. He said God has abandoned us. In many towns, earthquakes and hurricanes destroy every shack and church and hospital and school. Swaddling babies die. Is that the behavior of a loving, benevolent God, killing babies? What, Emile would ask, does a benevolent God expect people to do after everything has been destroyed?"

"What did God say?"

"Bo bourik mwen."

"Meaning what?"

"Emile said God was telling Haitians to kiss his immutable ass."

We broke into laughter.

I said, "Do you believe in God?"

"As a child, I saw the hopelessness in my own family and among our neighbors and on the streets. I would ask God *why*? People prayed and mourned and their lives didn't improve or became worse. Our mountains are eroding and our forests are disappearing. We lack municipal sanitation. We have too much hunger. Street gangs rule daily life. Air pollution. Cholera. Unbelievably, people still have faith and, amazingly, never lose hope. I don't understand them. Neither did Emile. He created the relief organization, he said, 'to help compensate for God's neglect and cruelty.' He was certain that God is a racist. God created Haiti but never visited because he realized he had made a 'grave mistake.' Emile said The Gut Bucket also is one of God's mistakes. All Black ghettos are God's mistakes. No, I don't believe in God. Do you, Ronald?"

"No."

"Were your parents believers?"

"No. My father said, 'God doesn't give a shit about niggers.' I believed him. Still believe him."

We talked for another hour, mainly about Emile's many years in politics and his clashes with corrupt leaders at every level of Haitian government. He had refused to run for president even after being supported by high-ranking U.S. State Department officials.

Although I had agreed to write a column about Emile's exceptional life, I was being perfidious by not telling Alphonsine all I knew, and, like a coward, I asked the standard journalist's question at the end of the interview: "Is there anything you want readers to know that we haven't discussed?"

She said: "I think we covered the major areas. Naturally, I want to know who killed my Emile. And why. I've telephoned the police several times, and they said no witnesses have come forward. It's the same in Haiti among the disenfranchised. They don't help the authorities, their enemies. We unintentionally hurt ourselves."

I remained silent, fearing I would incriminate myself. Although our reasons were different, we both wanted a witness to come forward. She wanted and deserved closure. I wanted a brave soul to break the chain of self-debasement in The Gut Bucket. But, I wondered, would the courage of one *honest* person be a symbolic gesture and nothing more? Would one witness mean anything in greater Black life? Would anyone care? How many more Dreadlocks were waiting in line? Would that lone witness be canceled for being a sellout and an Uncle Tom?

Alphonsine's expression showed that she recognized my perplexity.

"Well, Ronald, let's go to the warehouse, then to the airport," she said. "You'll see some of Emile's work firsthand."

I did not want to risk having Dreadlocks follow us in Alphonsine's car, so I was relieved when she readily agreed that we would use my truck.

"I want to see where my Emile was killed," she said as we drove from the parking lot. "Take me there after we visit the warehouse and airport."

"Are you sure you want to go there?" I asked,

checking my mirrors.

"Ronald, if you're concerned about my female fragility and vapors, please don't forget that I'm a Haitian woman from the lower class. Pain and suffering are our constant companions and a source of pride for many of us. Think of that: Pain and suffering are a source of pride. Many American Blacks also take pain and suffering as a source of pride."

She was right and I changed the subject.

"The best time to go to this place is early morning before the crowd," I said. "I could pick you up tomorrow at seven-thirty."

"Fine. It's what I must do."

20

I had never seen anything like Emile's warehouse even though I had spent several years covering hurricanes and humanitarian efforts in Florida, Louisiana and Texas. More than two hundred volunteers labeled, packed, stacked and loaded supplies. I followed Alphonsine as volunteers stopped their work to applaud and thank her for the relief mission.

"They love you," I said as we entered sunlight.

"Actually, they love Emile."

At the airport, I waited in the lobby while she went into an office and signed documents. Minutes later, we left the terminal and stood under a shelter on the tarmac. Shoulder to shoulder, we watched a B727-200 cargo plane lift off for Toussaint Louverture International Airport near Port-au-Prince. I nearly choked up as I watched the landing gear retract and as the plane banked and rose over the Atlantic.

Alphonsine looked at her watch, then skyward.

"It will land in Haiti in two hours," she said. "Many will rejoice and give thanks to Papa Legba."

I tossed and turned that night, remembering Alphonsine's peaceful expression as she watched the plane gain altitude and disappear. At one point, I walked onto the patio and stared at the moon over the water until the reality of doom hit me. If Dreadlocks saw me with Alphonsine the next day at the spot of her husband's murder, he would link us and see her as another mortal threat.

I went back inside to my office and cleaned the S&W. Afterward, I returned to bed. Staring at the ceiling, I realized that I did not know when Dreadlocks routinely came to the pool parlor, and I worried that we would face him. If I thought Alphonsine's safety was threatened, I would shoot Dreadlocks on the spot.

21

When I arrived at Alphonsine's home the next morning, she was dressed casually and wore a wide-brimmed hat and dark sunglasses. Amused by my surprise at seeing her out of professorial attire, she led me to the breakfast nook where we enjoyed coffee, eggs and plantains. I gave her my version of life in The Gut Bucket and specifically at the Mall of African Peoples.

"Emile said it was like so many places in Port-au-Prince," she said. "And people there know who doesn't belong."

"Why do you really need to go there?"

"Ronald, as you all do here in the States, let's call it closure."

"I understand. Still, it's not a safe place to be – ever."

"Of that I'm certain," she said, proffering her arm

toward the door. "Shall we?"

"If things get out of control, please let me handle it," I said.

"Indeed."

As we approached the mall parking lot, I scanned the area to identify potential trouble. Alphonsine touched my arm.

"Don't torture yourself. We have a saying: 'You don't have to look far for the truth to be revealed.' Do you understand those words?"

"I think so," I said, wondering if she had been playing me along, that she knew I had witnessed Emile's killing. Would she know that Dreadlocks is the killer when she sees him? Did she possess that Creole spirituality I heard so much about while in Haiti?

I parked on the street near the gas station because I did not want mall regulars to see Alphonsine getting out of my truck with me.

"This is it," I said.

"I've never been here but it's familiar."

"Why would you have come here?"

"Ronald, many of the children are talented artists, and they need teachers and mentors. I saw some of their work at the museum's youth exhibit last year."

She looked around the parking lot a long while, and as she opened the door and stepped onto the pavement, I touched my gun. Even before I exited the truck, she had crossed the street and was marching to the spot where Emile was killed.

I followed, keeping several yards between us. She stopped at the spot, removed her sunglasses and glanced around the lot. When her eyes rested on me, I felt like a criminal at the scene of the crime, and I wanted to run.

She stared at the spot again and put on her sunglasses. As if it had never been there, the spot had blended in with the dust and limestone. I walked to

Alphonsine and stood as close to her as I dared

without our skin touching.

"Here," she said.

"How did you know to come to this very spot?"

As she was about to answer, we turned at the same

time to watch the school bus stop at the corner and

activate its signal arm. I lowered my face when I saw

Frida cross the street and walk to the bus. I had

forgotten about the bus stop when I parked near the

gas station. Otherwise, I would have parked around

the corner.

Adjusting her book bag, Frida climbed on the bus,

walked to the rear and sat at a window. She stared

forlornly at the area where Emile had died. Several

other kids near her were playing. I knew Frida

recognized me even from that distance because her

head froze in position, and I could feel her piercing

eyes. I did not move.

Alphonsine stared from me to the bus.

"I recognized one of the kids," I said after the bus disappeared, feeling exposed.

"The pretty girl with the Afro Lady backpack? How do you know her?"

I told part of the truth. "I spoke with her mother about how gentrification is forcing them out of their apartment."

"What's the child's name?"

"Frida Welch."

Alphonsine's expression brightened, and she stared after the bus.

"I remember her," she said. "Frida. We loved her painting. I even recall the name, *Sweet Joy,* and I still see the girls eating mangoes. I asked her if she knew anything about her famous namesake, Magdalena Carmen Frida Kahlo y Calderón. She did not, but she said she would read about her online. I intended to find this talented child, but, regrettably, I put it aside. Apparently, she lives nearby."

"Yes and I'll forward her contacts to you," I said, afraid that Frida would learn that Alphonsine was Emile's widow and would acknowledge witnessing the killing.

"Excellent," she said. "I came here to see where my Emile died, and I also rediscover Frida. We have a saying: 'What is meant to be will always find its way.'" She stared at the back of the pool parlor, which had no identifying markers. "That's the place, isn't it?"

"Yes," I said, hoping she did not want to go inside.

The morning sun and humidity had become nearly intolerable, and Alphonsine shaded her eyes, not showing a bead of sweat. I sweated profusely all over.

She said, "Shall we?"

We walked to the building and before opening the door for her, I looked at Dreadlocks' empty parking spot and was relieved. The only vehicles in the lot belonged to employees, delivery people and, of course, the ubiquitous bail bonds mobile office was there. Just then, Doris Myers' TV satellite truck pulled in and parked behind the basketball court.

The last thing I wanted was a confab with Doris, Bari in tow, in the presence of Alphonsine. I opened the door and we entered Cue Man. No one was in sight. Alphonsine stood beside me, our shoulders touching.

"Hello," I yelled. "Anybody home?"

Glancing at his wrist watch, Barkeep emerged through a curtain behind the bar.

"Y'all mighty early," he said, taken by Alphonsine's beauty.

He expected me to answer but Alphonsine spoke.

"This is a nice place for billiards," she said, looking around at the tables and cue sticks in their racks. Everything was remarkably clean, and I did not detect the usual odor of marijuana.

"Ma'am, this a pool parlor," Barkeep said. "White

folks play billiards."

"Please forgive me. Yes, a pool parlor." With that, she turned to me. "Shall we go?"

Surprised, I followed her out of the building. After several yards, she touched my arm and we stopped.

"I could see how Emile was going to redesign the establishment," she said. "It would've been a gem."

Doris yelled my name. I turned and there she was with Bari beside her. They came to Alphonsine and me and stopped a few feet away, Doris beaming, Bari giving me stink eye.

"Professor Pomet," Doris said, surprised. "I stopped by your office, but you were in Haiti. I'm truly sorry for your loss."

"Thank you," Alphonsine said. "If you call or email me, we can arrange a talk."

"I'll email you," Doris said, then turned to me, her expression and tone free of mischief. "Nice to see you again, Ron."

"Same here. So, what're you up to?"

"Commissioner Murray and the Ministerial League are holding their annual No More Guns March next Sunday," she said. "Logistics meeting in the barbershop."

"Ah, the temple of Black wisdom," I said.

My sarcasm was more caustic than I thought, making Bari and Doris roll their eyes. Alphonsine looked at the ground. Because I had an opening to vent, I took advantage of it.

"There have been twenty-three murders in The Gut Bucket this year, and this is just September. These same people march and pray every year, and the killings increase every year. Is anyone out there listening? Two things for sure: It helps Murray's re-election campaigns, and it helps the barbershop look like a good corporate citizen."

"May I quote you?" Doris said.

"That's between you and your producers."

Alphonsine cleared her throat, and I realized that we were spending too much time there, risking a face-off with Dreadlocks. As I was about to tell Alphonsine we had to leave, Bari spoke, surprising Doris and me.

"Mr. Clary, the preachers had one of those marches the week before my big brother was killed right over there," she said, her tone angry as she pointed to the basketball court. "A bullet went through his heart. He was eighteen. They were playing basketball, and he and *that* boy started arguing. They were in different gangs. I didn't know what the fight was about until later. *That* boy ran to a car, got a gun and shot my brother. He died before the paramedics got here."

Her gaze turned to the basketball court. I did not want to sound insensitive, but I could not let the opportunity pass without asking her about snitching.

"You saw the boy who shot your brother, Bari. Did you turn him in to the police?"

Alphonsine intervened. "Do you agree, Ronald, that this isn't the appropriate time or place to discuss a matter so sensitive?"

She was right. I had done something any competent investigative journalist would never do: attempt to interview a prime subject on such a sensitive issue in the presence of others. Alphonsine extended her arm toward me in a manner suggesting that we should leave immediately. Feeling like the ass I was, I nodded.

"Let's talk again when it's convenient for you," I said to Bari, handing her my business card.

She took the card and smiled without judgment. I was both surprised and pleased.

"We need to set up in the barbershop," Doris said to Bari.

Securing their equipment, they walked to the barbershop. No sooner had they entered the building than Dreadlocks drove into the lot, parked and got out. He was accompanied by Giant Thug, who wore a white wife beater and sagging jeans, resembling a boy who had grown up prematurely.

Dreadlocks saw Alphonsine and me immediately. He raised his sunglasses and stared at her as if appraising his next sexual conquest. He ambled to us in the way of a playa. I braced for trouble and felt the reassuring weight of the pistol on my leg. Giant Thug strutted alongside him.

"Never seen you around here before, beautiful sister," he said.

"And you are?" Alphonsine said.

"Trey Saunders."

I resented that the bastard used his given name.

"I'm Alphonsine Pomet."

Dreadlocks' reaction indicated that he did not recognize her name, meaning he was so self-absorbed that he knew nothing about her or the man he killed.

He turned from Alphonsine to me. "Nice piece,

nigger," he said, winking.

"We *must* leave now, Ronald," Alphonsine said, touching my arm.

"You know what I want, nigger boy," Dreadlocks yelled. "You know what I want."

As we walked away, Alphonsine said: "What do you possess that he desires so?"

Over the years, I had learned that in my role as a journalist, most people rarely answered sensitive questions with total honesty. They either held back, embellished or outright lied. At that moment, it was my turn to answer what was a straightforward question: *What do you possess that he desires so?*

I lied. "I have photos of him selling drugs."

"All cornered animals bite. Avoid that person, Ronald."

I followed her to where Emile died. She blew a kiss and smiled. We walked to my truck, then drove away without either of us looking back.

22

At home, I went into my office, stared at my computer and continued to procrastinate, obsessed with the witnesses' silence and needing to begin my Emile profile for Asa. In reality, the two matters were intertwined, but I had to keep them separated.

What could I write about the witnesses that I could professionally defend? It would have to be a truth that indicted Blacks – and myself. Although I had the alligator hide of a longtime opinion columnist, I was not prepared for the fierce backlash I certainly would face from Blacks and liberal whites for condemning my own people.

I read the newspaper online, looking for anything related to Emile's murder. Nothing. As I had done countless times, I watched my video, made notes and sipped bourbon. I was stuck like never before, a quandary for one whose raison d'etre was to write competently on demand. By 3 a.m., I had not written a salvageable sentence about Emile's life, and staring from the blank screen, to my notes and to the keyboard, I felt drained, then drowsy, then numb.

As morning sunlight shone through the window, I woke up, my head on the keyboard, my temples throbbing and my throat burning. I rubbed my eyes, rebooted the computer and checked email. Nothing important.

I fixed a huge breakfast of scrambled eggs, fried mullet, cheese grits, wheat toast and strong coffee. I seldom ate that much at any meal, but that morning I needed the security of a full stomach.

After eating, I showered, dressed in relaxed jeans and an old fishing shirt. I sat at the computer, sipped coffee and waited for inspiration that never came.

As I stood to get more coffee, an email arrived from Alphonsine. I was excited and apprehensive:

Ronald, I contacted Frida and her mother. I'm

visiting them at their home this evening. Frida asked

about you. She saw us together in that parking lot and

remembered me from the museum. Will you

accompany me to their home? – AP

The invitation stunned me, and I finished my coffee

to gather my thoughts before replying.

"Yes," I wrote ten minutes later.

"Will you fetch me at home at seven?"

"Seven it is."

"Mesi."

I took my mug to the kitchen, this time pouring it

half coffee, half Jim Beam. I went onto the patio and

watched the shimmering bay as fishing boats headed

out for incomes. Feeling vulnerable, I wondered what

Alphonsine and Frida discussed on the phone and

what they would discuss in my presence.

Will Alphonsine tell Frida and Terri that her

husband was the man killed in the mall parking lot?

Had Frida and Terri seen Alphonsine on TV or in the

paper? Will they talk only about art? Will Frida acknowledge that she witnessed the murder and that I had interviewed her?

Will I finally be undone by the very people I had grown fond of? In fact, I had grown protective of Frida.

The rest of the day was a blur until time for me to "fetch" Alphonsine. I had always loved the lyricism and exoticism of fetch, but on that afternoon, it carried all the eeriness of the Muslim Adhan. For the first time ever, I was terrified, not of physical danger but of the unknown and my emotions.

I rang Alphonsine's doorbell the next morning. She opened the door and came out dressed like the art professor. On her shoulder, she carried a large canvas tote bag filled with books and art supplies.

"Shall we go?" she said, amused by my surprise.

I offered and she let me take the bag as we walked to my car.

"Why do you *really* want me to come with you?" I asked as we drove.

"I want to give your essay some hopefulness, something that involves a beautiful, talented child, something that brings smiles to faces. If readers remember nothing else, they'll remember our beautiful Frida. If she's remembered fondly, Emile will be remembered fondly."

I had more questions, but I would not risk self-incrimination. In no way was I prepared for Alphonsine to know that I witnessed the killing and had remained silent. For the first time, as I stole a glance at her, I thought of destroying the video.

She interrupted my thoughts, for which I was glad, when she said that she had talked with Terri about her plans for Frida, how she had found an annual summer art program in Miami for the child. Terri loved the idea and wanted Alphonsine to tell Frida herself.

"You really think a lot of Frida's work," I said as

we neared the apartment.

"I was like her. I needed a teacher and a benefactor. My parents couldn't afford a teacher, and they didn't have the social standing to attract a benefactor. I taught myself by reading voraciously and haunting every place that had artwork where I could enter free of charge. I won't let Frida get away from me a second time. I can say without reservation that *Sweet Joy* is the work of a gifted artist."

23

When we arrived at the apartment, Terri opened the door seconds after I rang the bell. Frida and Justine stood beside their mother, both wearing floral print dresses. They made an attractive trio.

"Please come in," Terri said.

The girls stared at Alphonsine and me, giggled and moved aside as we walked past them. I went directly to *Sweet Joy*. Frida elbowed her sister and they giggled. Alphonsine came and stood beside me, our shoulders touching, the girls giggling again, making me suspect that they thought Alphonsine and I were lovers.

Alphonsine turned to Frida, surprising the child.

"Have you painted anything special since *Sweet Joy*?"

Frida took a deep breath. "I did a portrait of my father from a picture mom took in Central Park, and

I'm going to put it in the portrait contest at the museum."

Alphonsine said, "I'd love to see it."

"It's at school."

"You think I could stop by to see it?"

"You have to ask my teacher, Mrs. Kushner."

"My good friend. I'll telephone her."

"Please have a seat," Terri said. "May I get you all something to drink – root beer, lemonade, water, chardonnay, Coors Light?"

"Nothing for me," I said, dying for two fingers of Jim or Jack.

"I'm fine," Alphonsine said.

She and I sat on the couch, and Terri and the girls sat in old straight-back chairs.

"So, Frida, what have you learned about your famous namesake?" Alphonsine asked.

Frida glanced at her mother before speaking. Terri smiled and nodded.

"A lot," Frida said, elbowing her giggling sister. "She was Mexican and she had a unibrow. I love looking at her face. It's so beautiful. She taught herself how to paint. She had polio when she was a little girl, and she got hurt in a traffic accident. She was in a lot of pain the rest of her life. My mom bought me a biography of her. I read it twice. It's in my room. I can show it to you."

Justine laughed. "Frida's got a bunch of makeup for unibrows," she said.

We adults struggled to hide our amusement. Again, Frida elbowed her sister.

I asked Terri if she named Frida for Frida Kahlo.

"Sure did. When I was in nursing school at CUNY, we had a lecture on communicable diseases, and Frida Kahlo was one of the famous people we discussed who had polio. I loved her name."

"Well, Frida, would you like to spend the summer in Miami studying art with my wonderful friends?"

Alphonsine asked.

Frida clapped her hands. "Yes."

"May I record our talk?" I asked.

Terri and Alphonsine nodded. I turned on my phone recorder and placed it on the coffee table. I was beginning to fully appreciate Alphonsine's insistence that my column contain a set piece focused on generosity and love and friendship.

"Frida, why did you paint the portrait of your father?" Alphonsine asked.

"Because I miss him."

"Yes, personal loss, grief, has inspired many great artists," Alphonsine said.

I feared what might come next: I was about to be exposed as the perfidious bastard I was for withholding the extent of my knowledge of Emile's killing.

"A man shot him in Harlem," Frida said, her eyes filling with tears. "I painted it to remember him."

Alphonsine reached out and touched Frida's hand. "I'm looking forward to seeing your portrait."

She stood, grabbed the tote bag, which was on the floor in front of her, and held it out to Frida. "For you," she said.

Frida was overjoyed as she stood and took the bag. "Thank you, professor," she said, struggling with the weight as she returned to her seat. Alphonsine sat and Justine giggled. Seeing her daughters' joy, Terri nodded for the girls to go to their bedroom.

"I'll bring the paperwork for you to sign, and we should be ready for Frida to leave for Miami as soon as school ends," Alphonsine said. "As I said, she'll live with my husband's former business partner and his family. She's a curator at the Pérez Art Museum Miami. They have a lovely home in Miami Beach."

"Not to be ungrateful, but why are you doing all this for us?" Terri asked.

"Mainly for Frida," Alphonsine said. "I'm a teacher

in search of diamonds in the rough."

"I'm worried about Justine," Terri said, glancing toward the girls' room. "She'll be lost without her big sister."

"I'll work on it," Alphonsine said. "Ronald and I will leave now."

The three of us stood.

"Anything on the apartment search?" I asked.

"Nothing yet," Terri said. "I put in two applications."

"I'll be in touch tomorrow," Alphonsine said.

Terri led us to the door; I was eager to escape.

In my car, Alphonsine and I agreed to have dinner at Acai Diner on the beach. We were seated at a table with a view of white caps rushing ashore. I had been there a few times over the years and thought it was expensive and pretentious.

"I need to confess," Alphonsine said after we were seated. "I wanted to come here because many of my colleagues will be here. I've always found it easier for condolences in a public setting. It goes quickly because everyone wants to get away, and there's less performance."

"You don't dress it up in lace, do you?"

Our waitress was a white university student who recognized Alphonsine.

"Professor, I'm very sorry for your loss," she said. "I'm Nora Bowes. My father is Jacob Bowes. He worked with your husband on several projects."

"Yes," Alphonsine said, touching Nora's arm affectionately. "Emile was fond of Jacob. How are your classes?"

"So, so," she said glancing around. "Too much chauvinism in architecture. When I start my own firm, men will make coffee and clean toilets – if I hire any men at all."

"Perhaps we'll have some beautiful buildings again," Alphonsine said.

The three of us laughed.

"May I bring you all drinks?"

"Crémas for me," Alphonsine said.

"Double Jack Daniels neat," I said.

"Very good," Nora said and left.

"So, what's your impression of Frida?" Alphonsine asked.

"When I first saw *Sweet Joy* in the apartment, my heart skipped a beat. Hard to believe a child painted it."

"I'm going to buy it if she'll sell it to me. Emile was my first buyer. I'll be Frida's first. Being offered money for your work is magic."

"Not to be boorish, but how much do you plan to offer her?"

"One thousand dollars."

"Whoa! That's a lot."

"It assures her that her work has value and that she has value. Of course, it's an investment in the future of a great artist. And, Ronald, I'm not being purely selfless. I'll have the first important work by the great Frida Welch in my collection, and I'm going to ask her to sign it."

"Have you told her mother?"

"No. I also have a plan for Mrs. Welch."

"You've been busy."

Nora returned with our drinks and we ordered dinner.

"So, what's the plan for Mrs. Welch?" I asked, sipping my Jack.

"I've found her a new job in respiratory therapy and a three bedroom apartment that has a Florida room for Frida's studio. I'm telling her tomorrow. Only one problem. It's in Miami."

"Couple of hours away, depending on traffic," I said. "Terri has nothing here in Mangrove Shores, and she dislikes where she works. She wants to take her girls away from here."

"You adore them, yes?"

"I adore them."

"Wonderful. The creator of *Sweet Joy* deserves every opportunity to become a great painter. Mrs. Welch offered a terrifying insight. She said that 'raising children in Cedar Gardens is criminal.'"

From there, we discussed art and galleries in Haiti, and I was surprised that so many of them still operated given all of the chaos. Our food arrived and we ordered fresh drinks. As we ate and chatted, several of Alphonsine's university and museum colleagues stopped and offered simple condolences.

"Forgive my impertinence," I said. "What would you do if you knew who murdered your husband?"

She put her fork on her plate, considered me and folded her arms. "As a child of Port-au-Prince, I saw my share of violence and revenge like it is here," she said. "When I was seven, I hid behind a fern and watched a gang leader, Yves he was called, shoot a police informant in the head three times at point-blank range. I screamed and Yves saw me. He ran to me and pointed the gun in my face. I shut my eyes, prepared to die. He said, 'Beautiful girl, you have no eyes. You saw nothing. Repeat it.' I repeated it and held my breath. He said, 'Run along home. Remember, you have no eyes. If you talk, I will find you.' Scared like only a child could be scared, I ran home and stayed in bed the remainder of the day. I had to explain the source of my terror to my parents. They warned me to remain silent. If I talked, the gang would kill all of us. You're the first person outside my family I've ever told. I never told Emile."

"Why?"

"I was his *innocent,*" she said, smiling. "He fancied himself as introducing me to the world. In truth, there was nothing innocent about me. Well, except that I was a virgin when we married. A year after I witnessed the murder, I saw Ives' photograph on the

front page of *Le Nouvelliste*, our major newspaper.
He was a victim of Pé Lebrun. In the photo, the tire
was burning around his neck, and his hands were tied
behind him. He was screaming and struggling. They
burned Ives alive on the street in front of hundreds of
people. He had snitched on another gang member. My
father said, 'Allie, you have no reason to ever
mention that man again. His death will not make us
safe. If you talk, they will necklace me like they did
him and turn you into a sex slave.' Ronald, I have
much to accomplish and none of it involves Emile's
killer. It all involves the dreams and aspirations we
shared. It involves children such as Frida. We have
thousands like her in Haiti who need help. I will not
jeopardize that to satisfy my anger and ego."

"Even if someone brought you solid proof of who
killed Emile, you wouldn't go to the police?"

"What's solid proof? Photos? A handwritten
confession? I've seen the American legal system at

work, how the guilty with smart lawyers walk free, how justice dies in a web of sophistry, how the relatives of the victims languish with false hope. I won't be a part of that. It would insult Emile's legacy and consume too much of my positive energy. And let me tell you something else, Ronald. I have no desire to kill another human. It would not bring back my Emile, and it would dehumanize me and turn me into a creature Emile would despise. Do you understand? Do I surprise you?"

"No," I said, awed by her quiet outrage and loyalty to Emile. "Have you thought of offering a reward for information that leads to the arrest of the killer?"

"I thought of it but decided against it because I won't enrich someone for doing what they should do as a matter of justice."

"Justice? If you don't get justice, what about revenge? Don't you want your husband's murderer to pay?"

"Pay?"

"Yes, pay. His murderer should, well, should...."

"Should also be killed?"

"Let's call it just punishment. Ten eyes for an eye."

Alphonsine was about to respond when Nora returned. I gave Nora my credit card and she left. Alphonsine dabbed at her lips with her napkin.

"Exactly what do you want me to say? Before you answer, I must tell you that my initial anger has been replaced by a profound sense of loss. Do you understand?"

"I'll have to think about it," I said, trying to conjure up the right words, feeling intellectually outmatched.

She said, "Revenge requires more effort than I'm willing to expend."

I could not summon a logical response. What would I say? Eye for an eye? Tooth for a tooth? Perhaps revenge is not logical or reasonable, but I wished that she would show emotion and a hint of anger.

"Well, this certainly has been quite a day," she said, sipping the last of her Crémas. "You may take me home now. I have much to do."

She waved to a colleague, and Nora returned with my credit card. She gave Nora an air kiss and we left.

24

As we drove, I checked my mirrors for a tail and did not see anything suspicious. When we arrived at her house and parked, she did not move for a long while and stared into the darkness.

"If you need me tomorrow, I'll be at the university vacating my office, which will take a few days," she said. "Then, I'll vacate my office at the museum. Too many offices."

"You really are leaving," I said, sad in a way I had never been in my life.

"I'm really leaving."

She got out, and I walked with her to the house.

At the door, she said, "Thanks for a lovely time."

"I hope to see you again before you leave."

"Que sera, sera," she said, touched my arm and went inside.

I drove to my apartment, poured a bourbon and

turned on my computer.

Time to write.

I opened a new document and typed the slug "Emile." For two hours, I read and reread my notes. After that, I wrote with abandon, expressing everything cogent that came to mind that captured the essence of Emile's extraordinary life. I did not write a single word about the witnesses.

At three that morning, I plopped into bed with Alphonsine's "que sera, sera" ringing in my head as I dozed off. I slept deeply the remainder of the night, a real accomplishment for a lifelong insomniac.

When I woke, the sun was just rising, and I felt the best I had since Emile's murder. I dressed, went into the kitchen and made a pot of coffee. I filled a thermos with equal parts coffee and Jim Beam. I grabbed a chair, walked to the water, sat under a cabbage palm and drank coffee, enjoying the warm air that flowed over me. After an hour or so, the sun had become so hot that I headed back to my apartment.

Dreadlocks, Hoodie and Rasta waited in the lowrider at the corner. I stopped. Dreadlocks, who was driving, lowered his window and made a finger gun, fired and blew away imaginary smoke. The car lugged away, hip hop pounding. I watched the car disappear, realizing that real gunplay was imminent.

In my apartment, I showered and polished the pistol again. The normal thing to have done was to go to the police and file a complaint, but I could not do that without self-incrimination. *Normal* had not played a role in any part of my life in a long time.

I had entered the netherworld.

After cleaning the pistol, I checked email and found one from Asa: "Ron, when do I see a draft of *Emile*? Your loyal readers really miss you." He was exaggerating about my "loyal readers." Like any editor with a columnist on a long leash, he was anxious to see some copy.

I replied immediately: "You'll have it in three days. Mrs. Pomet will provide photos."

He came back: "My nigger! Can't wait to read it."

During the next three days, I stayed in my apartment and wrote, periodically going on the porch to watch a cruise ship. On the afternoon of the third day, I transmitted the column to Asa. Afterward, I walked on the shore for nearly two hours. When I returned to my apartment, my phone was ringing. It was Asa.

"You maxed it," he said. "I thought I knew a lot about Emile, but you got his essence. By the way, Mrs. Pomet sent some great photos."

For the next two hours, we discussed edits, photos and captions. Afterward, I went fishing down the shore from my apartment, catching several striped bass for the freezer. I gathered my gear and catch and headed back to my apartment.

At the curb, Dreadlocks and Giant Thug sat in the lowrider, the engine growling and rap music thumping. Behind the wheel, Dreadlocks rolled down his window and motioned for me to approach, which I did cautiously.

"Be at Canal Park ten tomorrow night with that video," he said. "By yourself if you know what's good for your fucking ass."

He rolled up the window and drove away. No longer able to postpone the endgame, I had to face him, and I knew that giving him the flash drive would not save me. During the remainder of the day, I sat on the porch and read the entirety of *Florida Sport Fishing* magazine.

With Asa's assignment completed and fate coming for me, I fell asleep that night without the aid of Jim or Jack or a magazine or a book for the first time in years.

25

Next morning, I showered, dressed and was at Canal Park at 8:30 to scout the area. Along with dozens of Blacks, many white people were already there taking photos as proof that they actually had been to The Gut Bucket, a dubious badge of honor.

A handsome teen, wearing a Miami Heat jersey and baseball cap, pimp-rolled over to four attractive teenage white girls. Using all the moves, he kept them cracking up as he broke into a Crip walk, mouthing his own tune.

A girl shouted: "He's doing the Snoop Dogg dance!"

The crowd cheered. More Blacks arrived, set up tables and placed sheets, blankets and quilts on the ground to display their merchandise. Barbecue grills were lit, and food trucks arrived, each selling a special cuisine.

I glanced around, guessing at the spot where Deadlocks would want to meet me, where we would be alone, except perhaps for a few homeless men and coke-headed hookers. I was certain the location would be where the lighting was dim, near the water, away from the recreation equipment.

Giant Thug would be at Dreadlocks' side to intimidate me or kill me. I would arrive early, around nine-thirty, and stay in my truck to observe them. As I waited, I would put my weapon in my right trouser pocket. I would walk to them briskly to show that I was unafraid, and I would keep my hand on my gun.

The moment I got out of my truck, a woman called my name. I turned to see Bari walking toward me, without Doris. As always, she carried video gear and a notebook.

"Well, hello," I said, determined to continue the cordiality I thought we had begun. "B roll?"

She nodded. "What are you to up to?"

"Checking on pollution in the canal."

She turned up her nose and looked toward the water. "Stench gets worse every day."

I kept the good vibes going. "Have breakfast with me. My treat."

She scanned the area, checked her watch and adjusted her load.

She smiled. "All right."

"Seashells Café?"

"I love their pancakes, thick bacon and Cuban coffee."

"We have that in common."

"My boyfriend and I unload our hangovers there."

"That in common, too."

Looking at her, I realized that she was about twenty-five years old. We drove my truck and chatted as we went. At the café, the food and service were excellent like always, and the river shimmered as dozens of pleasure boats headed out to the ocean.

"Are you shooting something special?" I said.

"Just wild art. The Bucket's my home, so I pretty much know what to capture."

"Do you still live there?"

"I live with my boyfriend in Roseate Estates."

"Who's your boyfriend, if you don't mind my snooping?"

"Lon Seidel."

"The WMGS eight o'clock anchor?" I said, certain that my face showed embarrassed surprise.

"The same."

"I wrote a column about his immigration special, and he sent me a profane email."

"I read that column and Lon's email. He said you were 'full of fucking shit.' His exact words."

We stared into one another's eyes and laughed about the irony of our enmity and the source of her stink eye. In that column, I suggested that Lon treated Cuban refugees like returning war heroes while demonizing Haitian refugees as escapees from Devil's Island.

"Lon sees himself as fair and objective, and you labeled him a racist. You pissed him off and hurt his feelings, which pissed me off."

"May I ask you an inappropriate question?"

"I'll ask it for you," she said, leaning in and lowering her voice. "How did this little Gut Bucket negress wind up living with a Jewish news anchor in Roseate Estates? I get that a lot." She sipped her coffee and waved to passing colleagues. "I was shooting video for a red tide fish kill story, and Lon was there interviewing a kayak rental owner ruined by the stench. We started talking and had a drink. That drink was the beginning."

"Do Blacks get on you about dating a Jew?"

"You kidding? And, yeah, Jews attack Lon for dating me. But he's cool. He says, 'Sweetheart, take love where you find it, and fuck what Jews and

Blacks say.'"

"Maybe I figured him all wrong," I said.

She giggled.

"I want to ask you about your brother."

"Been expecting it since I saw you at the mall."

"Are you OK talking about it?"

"I'm good."

"Do you know the killer?"

"Javon Green. I see him on the street sometimes."

"Does he know who you are?"

"Don't think so."

"Why didn't you turn him in?"

"Scared. He belonged to Canal Dawgs, and my brother was in the Mangrove E-Lights."

"What did your brother do to him to get shot?"

"Had a thang with Javon's sister and bragged about it."

"Damn! He bragged about it?"

"Like a fool."

"Why didn't you go to the police?"

"The Dawgs would've killed me and my whole family if they found out I snitched. The streets talk twenty-four-seven, then some. Excuse my foul mouth, Mr. Clary, when I say these thugs are vile motherfuckers, detached from normal society, no blood supply going to their brains." She sighed. "I want to chop Javon's head off, put it on a stake in the middle of the mall and let maggots and flies and crows feast on it…. But he's just one. A thousand more just like him in The Bucket. I can't kill all of them, so why kill just one and get the electric chair, the gas chamber, the needle or whatever they use to execute you these days in the Sunshine State?"

Driving back to Canal Park, I asked about her career plans.

"I love my job, but I want to leave Mangrove Shores and break into one of the mega markets – New York or Chicago or Los Angeles."

"Not Miami?"

"Just down I-95. Too close to The Bucket."

I pulled to the curb near the giant slide. The crowd had grown to more than five hundred.

"I'm glad you want to get out of here," I said. "It's an ugly, unloved place."

"I know," she said glancing at the multitude. "But you kind of forget about the ugly and unloved side when you see people having so much fun, eating, drinking and Hip-hop blasting. Best music ever. Even Lon likes coming here for the music. It's a celebration."

I looked at the growing crowd and considered Bari's description of rap being a celebration.

"Some rap is fine poetry," I said, "but most of it is forced rhyme trying to relieve pain…. It's not a celebration, Bari. It's a requiem."

"A requiem for what?" she said, surveying the festivity, then turning back to me. "Now, I remember.

You wrote a column about that, rap as a requiem. I was a senior at the university. Someone mentioned the column in class, and our photojournalism professor said you were just a 'sad, self-loathing Uncle Tom.' He called you 'Uncle Ron.'" She giggled.

"I know the professor, Dr. Keith Paige, the 'Race Man' who never challenges Black bullshit. Do you agree with him?"

"I did at the time."

"And now?"

"After reading your stuff since then and meeting you, I don't feel that way anymore."

"There's still hope for you," I said, elbowing her arm and making her laugh. "I'm not an Uncle Tom, Bari, just sad and pissed at the horrible things we do to one another.... Do you know how many rap artists have been murdered by their own brothers and homeboys? Tupac Shakur, Notorious B.I.G., Takeoff,

Jam Master Jay, Nipsey Hussle, Pop Smoke, Young Dolph, PnB Rock, Bankroll Fresh, Dolla, King Von, Mac P Dawg, Big Squabble, FBG Duck, Kory3x, Seewright, R3 Chopz. A short list. I can go on."

"Got it."

"Bari, you do realize that a lot of rap is misogynistic: bitches, 'hos, skeezas, gold diggers, sac chasers and chicken heads.'"

"I know," she said and grabbed her video case. "Don't worry. I don't have Nikki Giovanni's blind love for these beautiful 'outasight' black men she wrote about in that poem." She sighed. "Got to capture some action for Doris before it gets too hot out here."

She was trying to escape, so I touched her arm, stopping her from leaving at that moment.

"Besides the music," I said, "what do you think about life in The Bucket? I really want to know as a fellow journalist."

"Is this for a column?"

"I don't know. Certainly not anytime soon."

She let go of the video case and leaned back.

"Please don't use my name or other stuff that let people know it's me." She surveyed the crowd again. "Except for the music and the ribs, I hate The Bucket. I wouldn't raise a kid here. Every one of these bastards has at least one stupid sister pregnant or already has a child with her or another one. What kind of future is that for The Bucket? The babies, the killings, the gangbanging, the drugs, garbage everywhere. Right now, my dad's playing checkers, guzzling Seagram's and talking shit under a tree."

She wiped her eyes with a palm, surprising me by how freely tears came to this young Gut Bucket woman.

"I'm sorry," she said. "I still see my brother on the ground bleeding to death."

I did not have an appropriate reply and decided to

back off. "Take care of yourself, young lady."

"I want to tell you something. Minus that crap you wrote about Lon, I totally agree with your pieces. I don't tell people I agree because I don't want to be called a self-loathing bitch, a sellout or a traitor.... Mr. Clary, I'm just starting my career, and I don't want to be canceled from the git-go."

"Like me?"

She frowned. "We're so mean to one another. Petty, cliquish and tribal. Gang against gang, church against church, club against club, mulattos against darkies. Anybody who says it isn't true is a mullet-eating liar."

I rested my elbow on the center console. "It's hell being a pariah. If I could start over, I wouldn't write a truthful, negative opinion about Blacks. I'd stick to straight news. Period."

"That's really sad, Mr. Clary. I feel sorry for you." She paused a long while, then tapped her forehead in a manner signaling an epiphany. "I just realized that you're a hypocrite. You don't hate Black people. You actually --."

"What made you think I hate Black people?"

"It's all I've ever heard in The Bucket: 'Ron Clary hates Black people.' But after getting to know you, I think you love us in your own way. The stupid self-destruction pisses you off."

Her assessment surprised me and made me smile. Existence in The Bucket had made her wise beyond her years. I was pleased that she would not become an angry victim or an indifferent abuser of her own people like countless others had become for generations.

She pecked me on the cheek, exited the truck and walked away. After a few steps, she stopped and turned and stared at me through the windshield, seemingly wanting to come back to say something. Instead, she pivoted and struggled across the lot with her gear. For nearly an hour, I watched her film and chat with Black girls dancing to Megan Thee Stallion and Rico Nasty. She was a natural with the girls. As I drove away, her words – *you care about us, Mr. Clary, even love us* – rang in my ears. Was she right?

26

On Anise Boulevard, I parked in the shade of the live oak where Jefferson Mims was mutilated. I got out and walked to a spot where I could clearly see Mrs. Pierce unveil the plaque honoring the long-ago victim. Wearing a flowing dashiki dress and a matching head wrap, she spoke to a racially integrated crowd of at least four hundred. I took several photos of her with my phone.

Commissioner Murray's choir sang a stirring rendition of "Lift Every Voice and Sing," and the good reverend followed with a sermon about "Christ's love for the poor and the forgotten." Glancing around, I was certain I recognized at least three witnesses to Emile's killing.

After the event, I went to a gun shop outside of town, and I bought concealed carry pants. At home, I put the pants on and practiced drawing my pistol.

Then, I drove to my bank and removed the flash drive of the killing from my safe deposit box because I no longer wanted it out of my possession even though I had other copies.

Back at home, I went online and had an email from Alphonsine: *Ronald, the Haitian government is forcing me to sign documents in the home office before they accept additional supplies from our mission here in Mangrove Shores. I'll be flying to Port-au-Prince tonight. The good news is that Frida and her family are all set to relocate to Miami Beach. Perhaps we can talk after I return.*

I replied that I would contact her. Logging off, with a mere six hours before meeting Dreadlocks, I was unmoored like never before. Sitting on my porch sipping Jim, I watched waves crash ashore and gulls fight for food. Expensive pleasure boats and fishing rigs plied the channel, and I longed for such freedom on the open sea.

At eight that night, I dressed and again practiced retrieving the pistol. The drive in my truck to the park took about twenty minutes, and I arrived before Dreadlocks, parked and rolled down the windows to hear everything around.

Moonlight and slow-moving clouds cast the area in an eerie glow, forcing me to acknowledge that I was in the final minutes of the nightmare I had created by naively hoping that at least one witness would speak to the police.

A young hooker coke-walked to my truck and leaned toward my window.

"Hey, pretty old man, suck yo' thang real, real good for twenty dollars."

"Maybe Christmas," I said.

"Suck it now or never."

"Not in the mood. Terrible headache."

"Fuck you, sick nigga."

She gave me the finger and pranced toward the

mall. I looked at my watch, nine fifty-one, heard a rumbling engine and looked toward the cross street. Dreadlocks and Giant Thug, in the lowrider, parked at the curb and got out.

As I exited my truck and walked onto the grass, Dreadlocks strutted to within a couple of yards of me, Giant Thug beside him. I kept my hand on my concealed gun. Giant Thug looked from Dreadlocks to me, waiting for orders.

"You got that video, motherfucker?" Dreadlocks said, his arms over his chest.

"In my pocket," I said, wary of Giant Thug.

"Give it up, nigger. And your phone. Everything."

"You get the flash drive. Nothing else."

"Guess we have to take it."

"Don't think so."

"Can't have your Tom ass running around with that shit," he said, holding out his hand.

I stepped away, watching Giant Thug adjust his

posture for action. Dreadlocks nodded and Giant Thug moved toward me, pulling a Glock off his waist.

I whipped out my gun and fired two rounds, feeling the recoil as Giant Thug's face exploded in a spray of blood and flesh and bone. He fell hard onto his back, his torso quivering. Dreadlocks bent over the body and looked for the face that was not there. I aimed at him.

"Give me your gun and phone," I said.

"In my car."

Not believing him, I told him to turn his pockets inside-out. He did so without protest, and I did not see a weapon or his phone.

To instill raw fear in him, I stepped to Giant Thug and fired another round into the body, this time the chest. I knew that many people heard the shots, and I also knew that few, if any, blinked. Just routine gunshots in The Gut Bucket. Same for law enforcement. My cop contact told me that after Gut Bucket shootings, he often heard a white colleague utter something such as "just niggers shooting niggers" or "nigger down," meaning there was no need for an urgent response.

Dreadlocks gawked at the new hole in Giant Thug's body.

"What the fuck?" he said, backing away from me.

"Making sure that big ugly motherfucker's not playing possum," I said, motioning for him to stand still. "I ought to shoot him again."

"Damn, nigger, you crazy."

Standing in the semi-darkness, a gun in my hand, a body on the ground with my bullets in it, mosquitoes whining in my ears and a murderer standing in front of me, I had no regard for the sanctity of human life, Black or otherwise.

I knew that my killing Giant Thug had changed Dreadlocks' perception of me and of himself. I pointed my gun at his face and saw disorientation in his eyes and defeat in his body language. He was diminished, his world flipped upside down. He no longer was king of The Gut Bucket, and I believed that he was afraid for the first time ever.

"Step back," I said.

"What, what the fuck you doing?"

I motioned with my pistol, and after he had taken several steps, I told him to stop. I retrieved Giant Thug's weapon and tossed it into the canal. The splash made Dreadlocks blink and stare at the dark water. He glanced around for an escape route.

"Don't try to run," I said, aiming my gun at his face. "Walk to your car."

A bank of clouds migrated over, casting us into momentary darkness. I jabbed Dreadlocks in the back with my gun to keep him disoriented. At the car, I asked him where his pistol and phone were. The pistol was under the driver's seat, the phone in the dash cradle. I made him lie on his stomach, face down and hands behind his back, while I retrieved the phone and the pistol – the one he had killed Emile with. I put it in a front pocket, the phone in a back pocket.

"Stand up and take off your clothes," I said. "Buck naked."

"Come on, man."

"Do it or you're dead right now," I said, turning on the video and recording him.

He stripped, and I told him to sit on the ground and lock his hands behind him. I threw his clothes, shoes and phone into the canal.

"What the fuck?" he said. "My keys, wallet, credit cards, driver's license, phone. Everything gone, man. What the fuck?"

"Shut up," I said and ordered him to state his full name, home address, date of birth and Social Security number. Then, I ordered him to confess to killing

Emile.

After the confession, I said, "Now, beg me not to kill you."

"Beg? Come on, nigger. I'm not begging."

I nodded to Giant Thug. "Then say your prayers and join that big ugly motherfucker."

After he begged, I replayed the video. He shook his head and groaned at seeing and hearing himself as a sniveling boy. I kept the video rolling and told him to stand.

"Turn around," I said, motioning with my pistol.

When he was positioned as I wanted him, I told him to stop, and I exchanged my pistol for his, the one he had killed Emile with. I shot him in a buttock with it. He yelped and fell, grabbing the wound, thrashing and screaming.

"I'm going to bleed to death."

"You won't be missed. I'm making copies of this video, and if you ever threaten me again, I'll give it to the police and the press. And if anything happens to me, one of my colleagues will take care of it. You understand?"

"Yeah, man," he said, groaning.

I tossed his pistol into the canal, walked to my truck and got in. Driving away and seeing him suffering, I was pleased. But after several blocks, that feeling dissipated when I recalled that no witnesses had come forward to snitch, to excise a deadly malignancy.

Were they refusing to snitch because they were inured to Black-on-Black savagery? Had the savagery become normal? Was the silence *rational* hopelessness?

What would Alphonsine think of my actions? As a witness to Emile's murder, what did I owe her? I had not seen the wisdom in killing Dreadlocks and risking lethal injection at Florida State Prison. Would my actions be acceptable to her if Dreadlocks winds up like Yves in Port-au-Prince, dead on the street or a rotting corpse in a Gut Bucket alley?

Public humiliation, I concluded, was a death sentence for Dreadlocks. What would Alphonsine have done if I had told her the *whole* truth about Dreadlocks and me? I obviously did not know, but I found comfort in her words at Acai Diner: "I have no desire to kill another human. It would not bring back my Emile, and it would dehumanize me and turn me into a creature Emile would despise. Do I surprise you?"

Instead of being surprised, I was awed. She lived in a realm foreign to me, and I would not attempt to explain it in the simple language of a newspaper columnist with only a basal understanding of human motivations. I had killed Giant Thug in self-defense, and although I had not killed Dreadlocks, I had shot the bastard as revenge for Emile and for his many other Gut Bucket victims. Was it enough?

My thoughts and doubts raced. Did I have an ethical duty to go to the police? By not going to the police, how could I earnestly judge Gut Bucket residents for their inertia? *Damn*, am I ethically obligated to hand over my video of Emile's killing?

27

At home that night, I read an email from Asa asking me to come to his office the next afternoon. I assumed he wanted to discuss my "ass-kicking Emile column," as he referred to it, and go out for drinks. When I arrived, he bear-hugged me, something he had never done.

"You're getting rave reviews, even from that old curmudgeon upstairs," he said, sitting. "Just got word about two shootings last night in Canal Park. Cops think they're connected. Roger Jenkins and Trey Saunders. Gut Bucket gangbangers. Somebody blew Jenkins' face off and put a big hole in his chest. They found Saunders crawling and moaning in the grass by the canal, naked, a bullet in his ass. They got him to the hospital before he bled to death. I'd hate to be him after the news spreads in The Bucket."

"How does this involve me?" I said warily, like the

guilty bystander I was.

"Not to get into the habit of giving you assignments, but for Sunday, I want you to write a piece revisiting your argument that no-snitch has metastasized and is destroying everything of value in The Gut Bucket. How does that sound?"

"Great. But I'm not writing it. You're getting my resignation."

He jumped to his feet.

"You can't resign. You're my best columnist ever. I can get you a nice raise."

"Not about money, Asa. I'm sick of the absurdity, spitting into hurricane-force winds and pissing on ten-alarm fires. Nothing's going to change for Black people. We can't even figure out that we're discounted and despised by everybody. We'll never be accepted. Never. We're on our own. We *must* take care of one another. We have to change. There's nothing else. We have to stop letting pain and suffering define our existence."

He shook his head. "I know you're stingy, but you ain't rich. What're you going to do for money?"

"Revise my porn novel and self-publish it. Catch a Hemingway-size black marlin and take a few photos. Release it and get drunk with some old salts."

"Really lofty career goals."

"I'm done with the Fourth Estate. I stayed with it this long because I like working for you."

"Can't bring yourself to say you love working for me, can you?"

"I don't love anything…. Well, except fishing and swimming in the ocean and drinking bourbon on my porch. In that order."

"Come on, Ron, seriously. You just can't walk away from your column. Lot of people subscribe to the paper just to read you."

"Lost the outrage. I don't feel *it*. Do you know what the greatest mortal threat to a Black male is?"

I paused. "A fellow Black male."

He sighed. "When's the last time you had a piece of pussy? Don't lie."

"Hell, I don't remember. Over a year, I guess."

"You're truly a piece of work. Are you going to stay in town?"

"Nope. Leased a waterfront cottage up in New England."

"New England? You'll freeze your ass off. Why're you going way up there?"

"No more Gut Bucket bullshit."

"What the hell are you saying?"

"You heard me."

THE END